LORD TEDRIC
Alien Realms
A Star Original

Tedric now realised whose voice this was . . . it came as no great surprise. What he was hearing was the disembodied voice of a member of the darker forces – of an adversary.

Tedric felt his lips twist into a smile. In the years he had spent in this universe in conflict with these mysterious creatures, he had never been so close to one before.

'Tedric is no more powerful than any human being. He's physically strong, a fine warrior, I grant you that, but only a barbarian, a savage even among the denizens of the Empire. To come here as Tedric did can only be considered an act of foolishness. The difference between bravery and stupidity is minute. Tedric will not leave alive.'

Other novels in the 'Tedric' series by E. E. 'Doc' Smith

LORD TEDRIC

Alien Realms

E. E. 'Doc' Smith

A STAR BOOK
published by
the Paperback Division of
W. H. ALLEN & Co. Ltd

A Star Book
Published in 1980
by the Paperback Division of
W. H. Allen & Co. Ltd
A Howard and Wyndham Company
44 Hill Street, London W1 X 8LB

Copyright © Baronet Publishing Company, 1980

Filmset, printed and bound in Great Britain
by Hazell Watson & Viney Ltd,
Aylesbury, Bucks

ISBN 0 352 30770 6

CHAPTER I

Skandos and Tedric

He wasn't really here. Thousands of parsecs away, his body lay asleep in the warmth of a bed in a house on the planet known as Earth.

But he wasn't in that body now.

He seemed to have a definite form – arms, legs, torso, skull – but he knew it was only a comforting illusion.

He floated in the thin air above the snow-capped peak of a mountain so tall that the clouds spread out below resembled distant, flickering memories.

He knew where he was: the planet Prime at the edge of the Milky Way Galaxy. The world where the Scientists dwelled.

The temperature of the air was surely far below the level necessary to freeze a man to death, but although he was a man, he was not cold. Only the body can freeze – not the spirit, not the soul, not a comforting illusion.

He looked beneath him at the second figure present on the mountaintop. 'Greetings, Skandos,' he said. (Although in actuality he said nothing: this was speech without sound or true words.)

'Greetings, Lord Tedric,' said the second figure, a frail, hunched man dressed in loose, flowing green robes. The exact reality of this man was difficult to determine. Although he did not appear to be affected by the cold, his feet penetrated the blanket of snow to ankle depth.

This second man was Skandos, the histro-physicist; he was many thousands of years old.

'You sent for me, sir?' said Lord Tedric. As he expressed this thought – and felt it instantly communicated to the other – he was also remembering on a secondary level the frank exhilaration of his recent trip to this planet: a voyage through the depths of N-space unencumbered by ship or suit or even body.

'I hope your journey was an uneventful one,' said Skandos.

Tedric smiled thinly. 'As uneventful as such a journey can be.'

Skandos nodded. 'I would have come to you, but at my age such travel can be wearying. Then, too, I must consider my colleagues. A number feel that our conversations ought not to be conducted privately.'

Tedric understood what Skandos was telling him – that this conversation would be heard by all the Scientists. 'Is there any particular reason for that, sir?'

Skandos sighed. 'You would have to ask them. For myself, all I can tell you is that a certain faction of Scientists objects to your presence here.'

'My presence on Prime?'

'Your presence in this universe.'

'But I thought I was brought here by . . .'

'By me,' Skandos said softly. 'The responsibility, I have been informed, rests entirely on my shoulders. My colleagues are sometimes fearful. I cannot wholly blame them. Our adversaries are a powerful force. Some would rather run and hide than stand and fight.'

'But not you, sir.'

'No, Tedric, not me – but that means nothing. I could be mistaken. Among other names, I have sometimes been called Skandos the Impetuous. There is an element of truth to that charge. Unlike the facade we prefer to present, we Scientists are not wholly devoid of human frailties.'

'I only hope I continue to merit your trust, sir.'

'So far, Lord Tedric, you have. Your progress since you first entered this universe has been immense. For the first time in remembered history, our adversaries have tasted defeat. A mere skirmish, some might say, and not the whole war. Nonetheless, it was a triumph.'

'You mean Fra Villion.'

'I do.'

'But Fra Villion escaped. Moments before the destruction of the Iron Sphere, he managed to flee.'

'Into the red cloud.'

Tedric nodded. Skandos wasn't asking him – he knew. Tedric was not surprised to learn that the Scientist knew as much – if not more – about recent events as he.

'And what course of action do you intend to take in response?' Skandos said.

'The only one I can. Equip a ship of my own and follow Villion into the cloud.'

Skandos smiled with what appeared to be pride. 'You are indeed a bold man, Lord Tedric. I must give you credit for that. There is, however, a specific reason why I summoned you here. I mentioned earlier that certain of my colleagues are rather timid souls compared to you or me. It is their considered opinion that the time is not yet ripe for a venture as precipitous as the one you presently contemplate. The mysteries of the red cloud are profound. Your powers are perhaps as yet insufficiently developed to grapple with them.'

'Am I to understand, sir, that you are in agreement with this view?'

'Not necessarily. As a matter of fact, I originally argued quite strongly in favour of an immediate assault upon the cloud.' His lips twitched slightly – the start of another smile 'I was overruled.'

'Then what can we do, sir?'

Skandos beckoned with a hand. 'Come here. I will show you one possible alternative.'

Tedric descended until he stood beside the Scientist. His feet made no imprint upon the soft snow.

'Observe,' said Skandos.

Tedric glanced past his shoulder. A circular instrument the size of a pocket compass rested in the palm of Skandos's hand. The instrument's face showed a view of a planet swinging freely in space. From what Tedric could see of the surface past a layer of cloud, it was a forbidding planet, lacking oceans and pitted with large craters.

'What is it?' he asked.

'Tavera. The headquarters planet of the black knights of the Biomen – the *vemplar*.'

'Why do you show me this?'

'Because Fra Villion is there.'

'Then he has left the red cloud.'

'It was merely a gateway – for him.'

'And you think I should go to this planet – to Tavera – to confront Fra Villion there?'

Skandos shrugged. Again, the hint of a smile played at his lips. 'I can offer no opinion. It is an alternative – the possibility does exist. The final decision, however, is yours alone to make.'

'I understand.' The Scientists, he knew, preferred to avoid direct intervention in human affairs, largely in hope that their adversaries would agree to steer a similar course. 'I'll go,' he said.

'I rather expected you would.' Skandos grew solemn, pocketing the instrument in the folds of his robes. 'The challenge, however, is not one to be taken lightly. So far, you have confronted our adversaries on the relatively friendly grounds of the Empire of Man. Among the Biomen, you will be an alien – and an unwelcome one at that.'

Tedric nodded thoughtfully. 'You speak of this as a challenge. How exactly do you mean that?'

'In my opinion, our adversaries are fully cognisant of my ability to discover Villion's present whereabouts and inform you. I believe this is a deliberate attempt to lure you into pursuit.'

'A trap?'

'Yes.'

'How?'

'That I cannot guess.' A worried look spread across Skandos's wrinkled face. 'I have made certain calculations. The odds against your achieving success are considerable, but if you were to win – to defeat Fra Villion in his own realm – the significance of such a victory cannot be over-estimated.'

'And Fra Villion could undoubtedly tell us a great deal about the true nature of our adversaries. He must possess considerable first-hand information concerning them.'

'As much, one would suspect, as you possess concerning us, the Scientists.'

'Still, whatever the odds, I intend to proceed to the Bioman Sphere at the earliest possible opportunity.'

Skandos nodded and, reaching out with both hands, clasped Tedric firmly by the wrist. Tedric, in spite of the insubstantial form of his body, could feel the old Scientist's passionate strength. 'I can only wish you good fortune, Tedric.'

'Thank you, Skandos. Thank you for everything. I sincerely hope your confidence will not have been misplaced.'

'That will not be a problem, Tedric. No matter what happens in the future, you have already served us well.'

Then Tedric was gone. In the flash of an instant, he rose past the sky. Prime, the planet, was a tiny glittering orb shining in the void.

Tedric soared through the vastness of interstellar space.

CHAPTER 2

The Commander of the Corps

His name was Phillip Nolan and he was the latest in a proud line of Nolan sons and daughters who had served the Empire of Man since its inception. This latest Nolan currently held the title of Commander of the Imperial Corps of the One Hundred. Next to the Emperor himself, Nolan was the most powerful and respected individual among the many billions who resided within the boundaries of the ancient star empire. In spite of this, right now, as he sat in the cool comfort of his office in New Melbourne on Earth, working late into the night, Nolan could not help but curse the workings of fate that had brought him to this place at this time.

The sad fact was that Phillip Nolan was bored to the brink of death.

He was still a young man. In his twenties. The unchecked energies of youth surged through his veins. And yet what did his present existence amount to? Life in a chair. Imprisoned by four walls. Locked behind a broad desk carved from natural wood. Papers piled in front of him so high that he had to sit up stiff and straight in his chair to peer over the top of them. Reports to be read. Memoranda to be initialed. Orders to be signed. 'No!' he felt like screaming. This wasn't a life suited for a man of his years and <u>character</u> – a man of action. Give it to somebody else, somebody old, he thought bitterly. Give it to a man who has already seen the universe and decided it's time to retire to one snug corner. Give it to anyone, he thought, but not to me. I'm tired. I'm bored. I can't scrawl my name one more time.

It was at times such as these that Nolan almost regretted the crucial role he had played in the rebellion which had overthrown Emperor Matthew Carey and restored Emperor Randow to his rightful throne.

In gratitude for his deeds, Randow had rewarded Nolan with his present appointment.

I'll give it back, he thought bitterly. The first thing tomorrow morning, I'll visit the palace and tell Randow I'm finished. I'll start over as a lieutenant on some far-flung planet where the only piece of paper that exists is the arrest warrant I'll be carrying for some notorious space pirate.

Yet, even as he dreamed, Nolan knew full well that it never could be. The authority of the Empire was still far from secure. Randow, though a good and decent man, was not a strong ruler. The authority he exercised relied heavily upon the traditional loyalties of his subjects. Without the support of the Imperial Corps, Randow might well hesitate to impose his will and thus allow the Empire to sink back into the chaos that had gripped it during the long years following the Wykzl war.

So it's my duty to go on, Nolan thought coldly. It's that – and only that – which keeps me glued to this chair I've come to despise. Duty and loyalty. The one makes me scribble my initials and the other makes me sign my name.

The vidiphone on one corner of the desk was flickering. For a long moment, Nolan stared coldly at the instrument, willing it to silence. When nothing happened and the vidiphone kept flickering, he finally reached out and punched the receiver.

The comely face of his personal secretary, a young, blonde lieutenant fresh from the Academy, smiled tentatively back at him. Nolan was surprised. He'd assumed the girl had gone home long ago. He realised he wasn't the only one whose life was sometimes controlled by unwished-for duties.

He struggled not to snap at the girl. 'Yes, Lieutenant, I'm still here. What can I do for you?'

'I'm sorry to disturb you, sir,' she said quickly, 'but there's an officer out here who insists on seeing you.'

Nolan frowned. That was all he needed. 'Who is it now?' he said, his irritation returning full force. 'Not another damned pup lieutenant complaining about his duty assignment. If it is, you can tell him from me that we're not running an entertainment service here and that he can take his assignment and . . .'

'It's not a lieutenant,' the secretary said, interrupting gently. 'It's a Colonel Tedric.'

'Tedric!' Nolan felt a joyful smile steal across his face. 'What does he want?'

'He says it's personal, sir. I told him to come back in the morning but . . .'

'No, no, no,' Nolan said hastily. 'Send him right in. I've always time to see Tedric.'

Switching off the vidiphone, Nolan came eagerly to his feet and crossed the wide room. He held open the door, waiting impatiently for Tedric to make his way from the anteroom into the corridor. If there was any man in the Empire whom Nolan genuinely envied, it had to be Tedric. Tedric, too, had served during the rebellion, but Tedric had been too smart to accept any appointments afterwards. He had retained his freedom. And Nolan envied him that more than anything.

Dressed in the silver uniform of a corpsman, Tedric came striding down the corridor, one arm extended in front of him. Nolan stepped forward to meet his friend, and the two men shook hands, ignoring the difference in their ranks. Tedric was a huge mountain of a man with blond hair and grey eyes. He and Nolan had known each other since both were cadets at the Corps Academy on Nexus.

Nolan guided Tedric into his office and shut the door softly. 'Well,' he said, turning, 'and where have you been hiding these past few months? It took a lot of nerve on your part to go running off, leaving me here drowning in paperwork.'

Tedric grinned. 'I've been busy myself, Phillip.'

'Not on Corps business, you haven't,' Nolan said, in mock accusation. 'I agree that you had a stretch of leave coming after your last assignment, but I was beginning to seriously wonder if I'd have to have you rounded up and brought back in chains. Where have you been, anyway?'

'At Lady Alyc Carey's estate. As you know, she purchased a large ranch in Old North America. I've been helping her fix it up.'

'What do you mean, as I know? Nobody told me about it.'

'I believe Lady Alyc personally called and invited you to spend a week with us.'

'Oh, that?' Nolan frowned. 'Well, I was too busy. See that desk. The only thing that could pry me free from this place would be a fire. Who's at this ranch, anyway – just you and Alyc?'

'And her subwoman, Kisha. Surely, you remember her.'

'I remember. A veritable tiger. Does she still like to claw people?'

'Only when she's agitated. And Yod Cartwright has been with us, too. He was the young man who was with me on the Iron Sphere. I've recommended him for an Academy appointment – he's decided to be a corpsman rather than a pirate – but nothing's come through. Perhaps you could . . .'

'Help?' Nolan laughed. 'I never thought I'd hear you asking for political favours, Tedric.'

'It's not for me – it's for Yod.'

'I know that. I meant nothing personal. Allow me to have my laugh. I get damned few of them in this place.' He went over and sat behind his desk. Without regard for the consequences, he swung his legs and dropped his boot heels casually on the crowded top. 'But that still doesn't let you off the hook. If you want my opinion, it's high time I put you back to work.'

'I quite agree, Phillip. In fact, that's largely why I'm here.'

'I had a feeling.' Nolan nodded solemnly. 'So you still want to make a run at the red cloud, do you?'

Tedric shook his head. 'No, not the cloud. I have another objective in mind. It may interest you to know that Fra Villion has reappeared in the Bioman Sphere.'

'It's interesting but not surprising. What of it?' In spite of the casualness of his tone, Nolan had a good idea what was coming next.

'I'd like your permission to go in search of him.'

Nolan swivelled in his chair, letting his heels slide off the edge of the desk. He came to his feet and crossed the room. One entire wall was a broad window overlooking the skyline of the continent-sized city below. Everywhere Nolan looked, he saw bright lights burning and flickering like a man-made galaxy of a hundred billion stars. 'Look,' he said, turning away from the window at last and finding Tedric close behind him, 'are you really sure this is necessary? If Villion has gone home, it seems to me we ought to call it a victory for us.'

'I wish it were as simple as that, Phillip.'

'What makes you so sure it isn't?'

'Because Fra Villion came within a breath of destroying the Earth and the Empire of Man along with it. If we pretend to forget that and begin to ignore him now, the circumstances must work in his favour. When he decides to move again, we will be as unprepared as we were the first time.'

In spite of himself, Nolan found himself nodding. He remembered the events Tedric had mentioned and knew that he was right. When Fra Villion had first appeared in the Empire, he had been dismissed as a simple pirate. It was only with the advent of the Iron Sphere, a ship the size of a planetoid, and the development of the matter-scrambler, a weapon capable of destroying a planet, that his real motive – the destruction of the Earth – had been learned.

'What makes you so positive he will move?' Nolan said.

'Because I believe I know him. Defeat is not something a *vemplar* can accept. Even if he was acting only from his own motives, Villion would not soon rest.'

'And you believe he's not? You think someone else is behind him?'

'I'm sure of it, Phillip.'

'Who?'

Tedric shook his head. 'I couldn't tell you that, Phillip,

even if I knew. And I don't. The Scientists are convinced of it. That's evidence enough for me.'

Nolan nodded his agreement. He had never quite known how to react to Tedric's close association with the mysterious, god-like inhabitants of Prime. I can deal with the entire spectrum of human affairs, he thought, but when the heavens choose to intervene, I'm out of my depth.

'Then I guess there's no use in my trying to argue you out of this,' Nolan said.

'Not unless you wish to order me to remain here.'

'And if I do?'

'I'll go anyway.'

'Then let me just say this. You're one of the few people in the Empire I feel I can genuinely trust. I don't want to lose you, Tedric. The Biomen hate anything and everything human. If you go charging in there, demanding the life of one of their leading citizens, they'll exterminate you like a bug.'

Tedric smiled. 'I was contemplating a more subtle course.'

'What?'

He shrugged. 'It might be wisest to keep that to myself.'

Nolan looked hurt. 'Don't you trust me?'

'Of course I do, Phillip, but . . . why should I burden you with my thoughts?' He made a sweeping gesture, waving at the crowded desk top. 'You have enough on your hands as it is.'

Though not completely mollified by Tedric's explanation, Nolan felt somewhat better. 'All right,' he said, 'then I don't see how I can stop you. Maybe I'm just envious. I wish to hell I was going too. When do you want to leave?'

'As soon as possible. Tomorrow or the next day. Now that my mind's made up, I see no reason for delay. I'll need a ship – not a large one. A good tug will do. Nothing advanced. No Wykzl shields or the like. Defensive armament only. When I enter the Bioman Sphere, I don't want to look like an invading force.'

Nolan looked worried but nodded. 'I'll have my secretary

issue the orders before she goes home. You're not going alone, I hope.'

'No. Ky-shan will accompany me, of course. And Yod Cartwright. Since his Academy appointment hasn't come through, he has too much free time on his hands. If I left him here on Earth, there's no telling what kind of mischief he might get involved in. Also, if it's possible, I'd like to have Captain Juvi Jerome assigned to my authority. She was on the Iron Sphere, too, and she's a capable hand.'

'I'll try to locate her and . . .'

'That won't be necessary. She's here in New Melbourne. Yod has been keeping in touch with her on a regular basis. Trying to, anyway. She insists he's too young and inexperienced for her. She may have a point, but at least Yod doesn't give up easily.'

'I see.' Nolan grinned. 'Well, is there anything else?'

'Just one thing, Phillip. Wilson, the renegade robot. Do you have any idea where he is now? As far as I know, Wilson is the only person who has ever been to the Bioman Sphere and returned. If I could talk to him before I left, it might provide some advantage. Otherwise, I'm going in there blind.'

Nolan was smiling happily. 'Isn't that funny you should mention it?' He thrust a hand among his papers and drew out one sheet. 'This report came in yesterday morning. From the Vylo Sector. Wilson has been arrested. It seems he was indeed running that gang of pirates that's been operating in the area since just after the rebellion. The corpsmen who captured him have filed a list of charges long enough to stretch from here to the Moon and back again. Wilson hasn't changed, apparently. It took ten men to catch and hold him. They've got him in jail on a backworld he plundered. If the natives haven't hanged him yet, I'll see if I can have him sent here.'

'No, don't bother.' Tedric had an anxious look on his face and began edging towards the door. 'I think I'd better go to him.'

Nolan laughed. 'Wait a minute. I was only joking. Do you

really think I'd let anyone hang old Wilson? Naturally, Randow will have to pardon him. Wilson had as much to do with the success of the rebellion as anyone – including you and me.'

'It's not that I'm worried about. It's Wilson himself. How long do you think a backworld jail can hold him? Do me a favour, Phillip. Send a transmission at once. Tell your corpsmen to double the guard on Wilson. Watch him day and night. Tell them to put him in irons if necessary. I'll be leaving at noon. Get me that ship. This might be my only chance.'

Nolan was laughing so hard that he failed to see Tedric leave. When he finally looked up and realised his friend had gone, he felt suddenly lonely.

With a sigh, he tapped the vidiphone on the desk. The lieutenant's pretty face beamed back at him.

'Sir?' she said.

'Come here a moment, please. I have a set of orders I want you to get out right away.'

Then, leaning back in his chair, he closed his eyes and tried not to feel bored again right away.

CHAPTER 3

Renegade Robot

Robot KT294578 crouched on the dirty floor of the cell, wrists and ankles securely bound in iron bracelets, and glared fiercely at the two fuzzy cheeked Corps lieutenants who knelt at the opposite end of the room, quietly playing cards.

'Hey,' said KT294578, trying to growl. 'This is a damned outrage, I'm telling you. This is a violation of every precept set forth in the Declaration of the Rights and Privileges of All Things Human.'

The younger of the two lieutenants looked up from the cards in his hand and shook his head. 'I'm afraid not, Wilson. We checked that out. Since you're not human, the declaration does not apply.'

'How do you know I'm not human?' The robot sprang angrily to his feet and lunged forward, but the chains attached to the wall held him fast. He shook his wrists, rattling iron. 'If I was free, I swear I'd break both of you in half. I may be a robot, but I'm as human as any man, and nobody has ever said differently and lived to boast of it.'

'We apologise,' said the second lieutenant, playing a card. 'If you say you're human, then you're human. Maybe that's why the Commander ordered you chained up. Maybe he didn't want the locals to stretch your human neck.'

'Do you know what you are?' the robot said. 'You're cowards – both of you. I thought corpsmen were supposed to be an elite – brave, courageous, bold. Come on. Let me loose. Give a man an even break. Show your mettle.'

Both lieutenants shook their heads. 'Nothing doing, Wilson. Our instructions are to keep you chained up tight till Colonel Tedric arrives.'

'Oh, sure,' said KT294578. He pretended to relax, sitting again. 'You poor saps,' he said feelingly.

The first lieutenant glanced up. 'What's that supposed to mean?'

'It means Colonel Tedric, that's what. Don't tell me you don't know. A born sadist. The cruelest man in the Empire. Tedric's going to kill me when he gets here and you two are going to have my blood on your hands. He won't give me a chance. The man has a mean streak four parsecs long. Hey – ouch!' The robot gripped his right leg. 'I've got a cramp in my thigh. It's killing me. You've got to let me loose now.'

The lieutenant yawned, playing another card. 'Don't bother, Wilson. We've heard your stories a hundred times. Cramp or no cramp, you're not getting loose till the Colonel gives the word. And if you don't shut up, we might just help him put you out of your misery.'

KT294578 spat. Then, chuckling all at once, he shrugged his shoulders. After all, what was the point of getting angry?

That, of course, was the focus of the problem – his problem. And not just anger either, but every other human emotion from total love to utter hate with a thousand and more stops between. Of all the robots ever built, only one – KT294578, or Wilson, as he now called himself – had ever possessed such things as emotions. If he was now a notorious criminal – and Wilson had never denied that was exactly what he was – he believed it came from the simple fact that he carried a human heart trapped in a machine body. Who could long remain sane under those circumstances?

One of the last robots to be built before the collapse of the industry, Wilson closely resembled a human being. Only his cold, smooth, passionless face, as unmarked as a baby's, revealed his true identity. He was at least five hundred years old, but the first part of his life he could recall only as a vague blur. He assumed he had spent most of those years as any other robot did, sold and traded through the various backworlds, passed from owner to owner, planet to planet, hand to hand. If at any time during that period he had suffered a major injury – the loss of an arm, for instance, or a leg – he would most likely have been sent to the furnaces and gone willingly, with nobody to grieve for a moment, most especially including himself.

For he hadn't been human. Not then. And now he was. That made all the difference in the cosmos, and he remembered exactly how it had come to be.

Although this was something Wilson had never confided to another soul, it was seldom far from his mind. If a normal man had been able to recall the moment of his birth, the memory would have assumed the same critical role in his consciousness as Wilson's memory played in his.

He had belonged to a married couple – colonists – Arti and Magi Javro. The two lived alone on a backworld in the Noradian Sector that had been studiously avoided by the large colonial groups that had left Earth during the time of the Scattering. The planet was not an especially fertile one. The winters were long and bleak.

But the Javros loved their planet very much – perhaps simply because it was theirs. And they loved each other, too. Wilson had not been aware of this at the time, but he later realised it was the only explanation that truly fitted.

He could see the two of them clearly in his mind's eye. Arti, husky, red-bearded, light-complexioned, with a gravely bass voice. And Magi, his almost exact opposite – slim and blonde and detached and cool-voiced.

Wilson could not recall how he had come into the couple's possession. He recalled arriving on the backworld in the middle of summer and labouring through a temperate autumn to carve a home out of the wilderness. He uprooted huge trees with his bare hands and raised and moved immense boulders. Arti designed and Wilson constructed a secure log cabin in a matter of two days.

Because of their isolated circumstances, the Javros treated Wilson more like a member of the family than a piece of chattel and he remembered and appreciated that, although at the time it had meant nothing to him.

Winter arrived without warning. One day the sun beamed like a yellow eye in the sky and the next a terrible storm roared and raged. Although some preparations had been made for the advent of winter, the suddenness and fury of this first storm caught them all by surprise.

With the storm came the beasts.

None of the survey teams had ever reported their existence. Wilson now believed that the beasts, for whatever biological reasons, hibernated during the warm months and emerged only with the cold. They were big, white-furred, red-eyed, sharp-toothed, two-legged flesh eaters. And there were hundreds of them.

With the first cold wind of winter, the beasts awoke and left their caves and went in pursuit of the scent of fresh meat.

Arti Javro said he was going out to collect additional firewood from the small shed just outside the cabin door. He told Wilson to follow him. Arti took less than two steps outside the cabin door and the beasts grabbed him and literally tore him apart.

Wilson sprang back into the cabin. He slammed the door and bolted the lock. Turning, he carefully told Magi Javro exactly what had transpired.

She nodded thoughtfully. Even then, he could almost sense the pain she obviously felt and yet she never wept a tear.

'All right,' she said finally, 'how many of these beasts did you see?'

'Hundreds,' he said. 'All just outside the door. They're white-furred, so the snow hid them till they moved.'

'Are you afraid they'll break into the house?'

He was already using a portion of what remained of their wood to board up the two small windows. 'Not now.'

'How much food do we have?'

'Enough for two months, Earth reckoning.'

'For me alone?'

'I've already taken that into account.'

'Then we'll simply have to stay here and wait for the beasts to leave.'

But the beasts did not leave. At least twice a day Wilson

peered through a narrow gap in the boarded-up window closest to the door and the beasts were always there, though at times he had to squint to see them clearly through the white haze of a storm. Undoubtedly, some did leave, but others must have come, for their original number never lessened. The winter was long and bleak. Storm followed storm, piling drifts high around the cabin. One month passed, then two.

At night, for warmth and because they had long since exhausted their supply of firewood, Magi slept with Wilson, her arms and legs encircling his body, her cheek pressed close to his chest, and while this was not the prime reason for what later happened to him, it was surely a part of it.

At the end of this period, although a small quantity of food remained unconsumed, Magi Javro was thin, drawn, weak, and easily exhausted.

'Do you think when spring comes the beasts will go away?' she asked.

He said, 'Yes.'

'And when will that be?'

'One month, maybe two.'

'I'll be dead. You won't. You don't have to eat but I do. If I stay here I'll starve to death and if I go out I'll be eaten alive.'

Wilson, a typical robot without emotions, simply nodded. What his mistress said was true.

'So we have no hope. I don't. There's no point in prolonging the inevitable.'

It was right then, just as she finished her statement, that it began to happen. Part of it happened. Wilson felt a strange stirring in his breast. Before he knew what he was doing, he said, 'You could eat me.'

He expected her to be disgusted, but she just shook her head, smiling faintly. 'I could but I won't.'

'Why?'

'It wouldn't be right.'

'Because of the taboo?'

'No, not really. I honestly think I'm way beyond that.'

He argued. He told her it made sense. With his flesh, she could last another month – even more. She could live till spring.

She shook her head firmly. 'I won't do it.'

'Why? It can't be wrong. I'm not human. My life is meaningless.'

'No.'

'Why not?'

'Because I love you.'

He couldn't comprehend that. Even though he was by now at least half human, the complexity of such an emotion left him bewildered. He excused himself and went into a corner and sat with his back facing her and pondered the meaning of what she had said.

Love, he thought. What is it? How can she, a woman, have such feelings for me, who is only a machine? No, no, it doesn't make sense. I can't . . .

He was in the middle of these thoughts when a loud noise roused his attention. It was the slamming of the door.

He looked up and saw that he was alone.

By the time he got outside, there was no sign of Magi. The beasts clustered in a circle, tearing at something unseen in the middle of them. Wilson went after them with his bare hands. He killed a dozen and wounded even more, but finally they drove him back to the cabin.

He waited there till winter ended. Spring arrived with the same abruptness as winter and the snow thawed in a great rush of heat. The beasts went away.

Wilson emerged in the pure sunlight. With his hands, he dug a hole in the damp ground and placed some of Magi's personal belongings – clothes, jewellery, a book – in the bottom. Then he covered the grave and lay on the ground and wept.

From that moment on, willingly or not, Wilson was completely human – inside, where it mattered.

He became an outlaw. Given the conflicting circumstances of his existence, he believed no alternative lay open to him.

In time, his activities brought him to the attention of the

23

imperial authorities. He was chased and hunted but never caught. In the end he did what no man had ever done. He left the Empire of Man and went to the Bioman Sphere. Later, he also visited the alien Dynarx and lived among them.

Upon his return to the Empire, Wilson resumed his outlaw activities, finding in the corruption of the latter-day Empire a perfect setting for his own designs. Somehow, more by accident than intention, he became involved in the rebellion that sought to oust Matthew Carey from the imperial throne. When the rebel forces defeated the imperial fleet in a great battle just beyond the orbit of Pluto, Wilson joined his fellow rebels and went to Earth in triumph. In the wake of victory, Wilson could have had almost anything he desired; wealth, glory, and position were his for the asking.

But what he wanted was none of that. At the earliest opportunity, he left the imperial court, took a ship, and went to the Vylo Sector in a remote corner of the Empire, where he immediately resumed his life as an outlaw.

Unfortunately for Wilson, the success of the rebellion interfered with his chosen way of life. Under the leadership of Phillip Nolan, the Imperial Corps of the One Hundred presented a real obstacle to any outlaw band. In time, Wilson was caught and arrested.

And now he was in jail here on his backworld, waiting for he wasn't sure what.

'Wilson.'

At the sound of his name, he raised his eyes. Lost in thought, he had no idea of how much time might have passed. The two young lieutenants had vanished. In their place stood a lone man – tall, thickly-muscled, blond – wearing the silver uniform of a corpsman. Wilson recognised this man from the time they had fought side by side during the rebellion.

'Tedric,' he said, with more real pleasure than he had anticipated.

Wilson came to his feet and went as far forward as his

chains would allow. Tedric met him at this place, and the two men clasped hands.

'So we finally managed to bring you down,' said Tedric, 'and put you where you belong.'

'Ah, it's a mistake,' said Wilson. 'You've got me confused with somebody else.'

'There is nobody else like you, Wilson.'

'You're only saying that to make me feel good.'

They laughed together and sat on the floor. 'And what about the others?' Wilson said. 'How are Nolan and Ky-shan and the Lady Alyc? You know, we had a lot of fun back then, when we were overthrowing an empire. I don't suppose I could talk you into trying it again.'

Tedric grinned. 'I'm afraid, unlike you, I've reformed. Phillip you must know about. He's the new commander of the Corps of the One Hundred.'

Wilson, smiling, held up his wrists. 'Yes, I do know about him.'

'And Alyc is fine. She's living on Earth and Kisha is with her.'

'Is that little she-cat as mean as ever?'

'Worse.'

'What about Keller? The subman. What became of him?'

'He entered the Corps. His wife is with him now. The last I heard he was chasing a band of pirates near Altair.'

'That bunch of amateurs,' said Wilson, with feeling. 'And Ky-shan?'

'Oh, he's with me now. I would have brought him along but I preferred to see you in private first.'

Wilson frowned tightly. 'Then I assume you're here on business, not pleasure. Those two young pups guarding me kept saying that Colonel Tedric was coming but they'd never tell me why.'

'I want a favour from you,' Tedric said.

'Not a confession, I hope.'

'No, just information.'

'If you want me to spill . . .'

'Oh, no. Nothing like that. This is something completely

different. You once told me you'd visited the Bioman Sphere. I want you to tell me everything you can about that domain.'

'For any particular reason?'

'Because I plan on going there.'

Wilson shook his head. 'The Biomen don't care much for visitors. The only reason they tolerated me was that I managed to convince them that, as a robot with feelings, I wasn't a whole lot different from them. If I'd been a normal man, I think they would have killed me.'

'I'm aware of the danger,' said Tedric. 'It's a risk I believe I have to take. There's someone I want to find.'

'Fra Villion.'

Tedric looked surprised. 'How do you know about Villion? Nothing concerning his real identity was ever publicised.'

'I know he's a black knight, a *vemplar*. My work requires me to keep track of possible competitors. I thought Villion was killed when the Iron Sphere exploded.'

'No, he escaped. We didn't publicise that either.'

'And now he's back home?'

'Yes.'

Wilson shook his head. 'Well, I really don't know what I can tell you that'll help. The Bioman Sphere isn't nearly as large as the Empire. There are perhaps fifty planets in the realm and most are largely inhabited by the primitive robots who do most of the Biomen's dirty work for them. The capital planet, Kleato, is an interesting place, one vast city, and I'd bet more than half their population resides there. Tavera is where you'll most likely find Fra Villion. That's where the *vemplars* make their headquarters.'

'What can you tell me about them?'

'Little that you probably don't know. The *vemplars* are a group of mercenary soldiers trained since birth in the art of combat, owing little loyalty to person or species. Since most Biomen are far too civilised to fight wars, the *vemplars* expend most of their energies on things like private duelling. If a war ever did break out – between the Biomen and the Empire, for instance – you wouldn't find a better fighting force, but as it is, they're largely anachronisms, tolerated less for what they are and more for what they once were. If you're wondering what Villion was doing in the Empire, you're not alone. I couldn't figure it out either. Somebody or something must have hired him. But who? And for what?'

'Then tell me this,' said Tedric. 'If you were me and wanted to find Villion, how would you proceed?'

'I don't have any idea. If you try to reach Tavera, they'll kill you on sight. If you don't go there, you may survive but you'll probably never see Villion either. The *vemplars* seldom associate with the other Biomen.'

'What about the Biomen? How do they look? Do they resemble humans in physical form?'

'Some do and some don't. The Biomen can assume any physical form they desire.'

'Villion looked like a great black beast.'

'That's a favourite form among the *vemplars*.'

Tedric nodded. 'I asked because I was considering using a disguise.'

Wilson clucked his tongue sadly. 'A good idea but it won't work.'

'Why?'

'There aren't more than a few hundred *vemplars*. They all know each other. They'd spot you for a fake in an instant.'

Tedric sighed. 'Then maybe the whole enterprise is hopeless.'

Wilson got a sudden gleam in his eye. 'And maybe not. I just thought of something that might help.'

Tedric looked up eagerly. 'What?'

'After I left the Bioman Sphere, I went next door and stayed with the Dynarx.'

'Yes, I remember your saying that.'

'Well, I wasn't the only outsider among them. There was also a former *vemplar* named Pal Galmain. He was hardly typical of his kind, and since I wasn't either, we became friends of sorts. It might be possible to get him to help you.'

'Why?'

'Because he was driven into exile by the other *vemplars* and has no great love for a number of them. One of those I

27

remember him mentioning was none other than Fra Villion. The name stuck in my mind and, when I heard about Villion being here, I remembered he was the same person.'

'The Dynarx, huh?' Tedric grinned. 'That ought to make an interesting trip. Especially with Ky-shan on board.'

Wilson nodded. The Wykzl were ancient enemies of the Dynarx. 'Of course,' he said, 'you couldn't possibly do this by yourself.'

Tedric raised an eyebrow. 'No?'

'Pal Galmain would never trust a stranger. He's still that much of a *vemplar*. With me along, though, you might possibly have a chance.'

'Are you making an offer?' Tedric said, with a grin.

Wilson held up his wrists and shook the chains. 'It's either that or this. I'll take that.'

Tedric stood. 'I'll arrange for your immediate release.' At the cell door, he paused. Reaching into a pouch on his belt, he drew out a folded sheet of paper and tossed it to Wilson. 'You might want to look at this while I'm gone.'

'Why? What is it?' Wilson picked up the paper in his hands and started to unfold it.

'Your pardon from Emperor Randow.'

Wilson spluttered explosively. 'Why, you . . . you tricked me. You knew all along I was going to be set free.'

Tedric grinned. 'Want to change your mind?'

Wilson thought it over, then grinned back. 'Hell, no. If I stay in the Empire, pardon or no pardon, I'll just end up back here again in a few months. The only happy time in my whole life was spent with the Dynarx. No, I'll take you that far at least.'

'I ask nothing more,' said Tedric, and he went on out.

CHAPTER 4

Tavera

As the robot swivelled on its wheels to leave the room, Matthew Carey found he could no longer resist the impulse of his anger. He shot his foot forward in a swift savage kick that caught the robot squarely in the middle of its aluminium rump and sent the half human-sized machine sprawling through the doorway.

Carey stepped forward and, with a final burst of anger, slammed the door shut. Alone, he looked at his hands and saw that they were trembling.

'Damn it,' he said aloud, as angry with himself as he had been with the robot. I'm losing control, he thought, taking my rage out on a poor dumb machine.

With a weary sigh, he dropped into a chair and put his hands in his lap to stop them from shaking.

The problem wasn't simply anger, he knew; it was boredom, frustration, humiliation, and rage. He was going slowly crazy trapped in this damned place. Long ago he'd ceased counting the days that had passed since his arrival here in the fortress of the *vemplars* on the planet Tavera in the Bioman Sphere. Such a tabulation probably meant nothing anyway, since he was sure the days were longer here than on Earth, or at least they seemed that way; boredom, he knew, could play that trick, too.

There was a time, not long ago, when Matthew Carey had reigned as an emperor. Even before that, he'd been heir to the most powerful fortune in the Galaxy.

And what was he now? Where was he now? A prisoner in this one damned room. And who did he have to blame for that? His old enemy, Phillip Nolan? The mysterious corpsman, Tedric? Or Fra Villion?

Villion, yes, to be sure, but more than that Carey blamed

himself. He had been a damned fool, he realised. Blind ambition and insatiable greed had brought him from the summit to the abyss. He regretted everything he had done. By the Lords of the Universe, how he regretted it. But regret would not help him now. It wasn't enough to set him free from this prison.

Through the large glass window above the bed, he could hear the steady whistling noise of the *vemplars* exercising in the courtyard below. Driven by his own boredom, he left his chair and went over to watch. There were several dozen down there. From this height, they all looked the same, dressed in their black jumpsuits and capes. The *vemplars* were fencing with whipswords, the personal weapon that each one carried. For a long while, Carey watched as two-by-two the *vemplars* spun through the air like crazed dancers, their weapons slicing and whistling. Carey's head began to ache from watching the spectacle. Turning away, he shrugged. What did it matter? They were out there most days. He'd seen all this before. A moment of curiosity sent him briefly back to the window. Was Fra Villion down there? He stared but of course it was impossible to tell for certain. He hadn't seen Villion since his arrival. It was no wonder he felt like a forgotten man.

Of course, Villion had saved his life back on the Iron Sphere. No matter what happened, he was grateful for that. Villion could easily have left him to die with the rest of the crew when the matter-scrambler exploded. Why hadn't he? For Carey, this was a mystery worth pondering. It wasn't loyalty; it wasn't concern. Villion knew nothing of such emotions. The only reason he could have had for saving Carey was to make use of him later. But how? That was the part of the mystery he had so far failed to solve.

He went back to the chair and sat down. He wondered what time it was. Early, he decided. The meal the robot had brought – and which still lay untouched on the table – appeared to be breakfast. That meant he had nothing to look forward to except lunch in a few hours. Each day after lunch the robots took him outside to the courtyard – the *vemplars* were gone by then – for his daily exercise. Sometimes he ran or jumped and stretched his muscles, but usually he simply walked, pacing back and forth, back and forth. The sun in the pale pink sky was a blood red disc. From what he had seen of Tavera, the planet itself was no hospitable environment. The tiny slice of land near the castle was ugly, dusty, cratered, a large cool desert.

Suddenly, looking up, he realised that the door was open. He stood, remembering how he had slammed it shut behind the robot.

Then he saw her. She stood next to the window, her back against the wall, her arms folded beneath her breasts, her eyes glinting with amusement. In spite of himself, Carey jumped in surprise.

She laughed. 'Why, Matthew, what's wrong? I didn't frighten you, did I?'

'Lola?' he said.

She crossed the room. 'Nobody else.'

She was indeed a beautiful woman. Even under these rather disturbing conditions, Carey felt entranced by her beauty. Blonde, grey-eyed, as perfectly formed as a piece of classical sculpture, Lola Dass wore the black cape and jumpsuit of a *vemplar*. The leather-like fabric of the suit clung to her figure like a second skin.

'Have you been here all along?' he said.

She nodded. 'Since the Iron Sphere.'

'I woke up in this room. I don't know how I got here. Do you?'

'Fra Villion brought us.'

Carey felt a burst of anger. 'I haven't seen him. Where is he? I'm a prisoner here.'

She cocked her head at the open door. 'It wasn't locked.'

He knew she was taunting him. No, the door was not locked but, when he'd tried to leave, an invisible forcefield in the corridor had driven him back into the room.

'What does he want with me? I assume you're still with him. Why is he holding me prisoner here?'

'Why, Matthew.' She laughed, reaching out with a hand

31

and drawing her fingers slowly down his cheek. 'You don't act pleased to see me. I thought we were old friends.'

He tried to remain cool to her touch. 'I said, what does he want?'

She shrugged, turning away from him, as if bored by his stubbornness. 'Why don't you ask him that?'

'I would if I could.'

She paused in the doorway and beckoned with a finger. 'Then come on. It's why I'm here. He asked me to bring you to see him.'

Carey wasn't even mad at her for failing to tell him until now. 'Well, it's about time.' He felt suddenly bold. 'When I see him, I'm going to demand he send me home.'

'I wouldn't do that if I were you.'

'Why?'

'He might take you literally.'

'What does that mean?'

'It means he might decide to send you home, all right – and forget the ship.' Her words chilled him. Or maybe it was the tone of voice she used – as cool and detached as a sliver of ice.

She waved him through the door. As they moved through the shadowy fortress – the forcefield, naturally, was no longer in effect – he tried to memorise their route for future use. He grew confused almost right away. Up two flights of stairs and down one. Turn left into a broad hallway and right into a much narrower one. Count four doors on the left and then into a large unfurnished room. Through that and up another flight of stairs.

At the top, Lola Dass knocked softly on a door.

'Enter,' said a deep voice that Carey instantly recognised as Fra Villion's.

Lola opened the door and stepped inside. Carey brushed past her. Fra Villion sat in a big chair. He was as huge as a bear and covered from neck to toes in thick black fur. His smooth face was a tumult of bright rainbow splashes, and his tiny eyes burned with dark, hidden emotions.

Any boldness Carey might have felt evaporated in the presence of Villion.

'Sit,' Villion ordered.

The room was sparsely furnished. Carey found a tiny armless wooden chair and sat down stiffly. A fire burned in a brick fireplace, the flames casting bright patterns on the Bioman's face.

'What do you want with me?' Carey said, when he could bear the silence no longer. His tone was anything but threatening, however.

Villion met his gaze. 'When I chose to save your petty life aboard the Iron Sphere, I fondly hoped that you might prove of some future value. That time, I believe, has now arrived.'

Carey shook his head as vigorously as he could manage. 'No. I won't do it. I won't help you. I'm through being used. Kill me if you want but I won't do it.'

Villion smiled grimly. 'Come, Carey, are you being fair? I saved your life even after you had betrayed me. Don't think I've forgotten how you led the one called Tedric to my door. What if he had slain me in the duel we fought? It was Lola who came to my rescue then, not you. If I had perished, how deeply would you have mourned?'

'Tedric forced me to help him,' Carey said, hating his own voice even as he spoke. 'And I warned you.'

'Perhaps. But, in that case, you must feel some degree of bitterness towards Tedric. After all, didn't he use you as you claim I also did? All I offer is the opportunity to exact an equitable revenge. Surely, you cannot be opposed to that.'

'Revenge against Tedric? How?'

'I wish you to spy upon him.'

'Where? Are you sending me home?' He would do anything to get away from this damned place.

Villion shook his big head. 'Fortunately, that will not prove necessary. Tedric, it appears, has chosen to come to us.'

'Tedric? Here? On Tavera?'

'Not yet, but soon. Those I represent have kept me

33

informed of his travels. His actual designs, however, are somewhat more obscure. That is why I have need of you.'

'What can I do? Tedric isn't exactly a friend of mine.'

'At the present moment, Tedric is visiting among the Dynarx. Are you familiar with the breed?'

'I know they're the fourth advanced species in the Galaxy, but that's about all. There's been little contact between them and the Empire.'

'Which makes Tedric's visit there even more interesting. The Dynarx are a crude, graceless, foul race, but one not without certain talents. Nonetheless, I doubt that Tedric will find what he seeks among them. The Dynarx are quite disinterested in the conflicts of others. Still, when you go there, you will be able to report more definitively.'

'How do you plan to get me there?'

'Oh, by conventional means. I have requisitioned a ship for your use. The navigational systems have been set to carry you to Tedric. Find him and explain that you've recently escaped my clutches and wish to offer your services in his cause.'

Carey laughed at the transparency of Villion's plan. 'Do you really expect Tedric to believe that?'

'Whether he believes it is of little consequence. He will not perform the one logical act that might save him and that is to take your miserable life. Most normal human beings – including Tedric – possess compunctions about killing, even when murder is the only wise course. A pity for Tedric but good fortune for me. Alive, whether trusted or not, you will serve my ends.'

'And what exactly are those?'

'To observe Tedric and inform me of his every word and deed. Tedric represents an unstable, uncertain force in this rather predictable universe. I need to know exactly what he's doing at all times.'

'How am I supposed to make these reports? I don't think Tedric will let me walk in with a communicator in my hand set to your private frequency.'

'A radio won't be necessary. I have other, more direct

means in mind.' Villion stood, a smile clinging to his lips, and crossed the room. He loomed above Carey like a stark, natural force. 'There is a certain ancient technique known to us *vemplars*. Let me see your eyes.'

Frightened all at once, Carey tried to look away, but his head turned upward in spite of himself. Unwillingly, he gazed directly into Fra Villion's dark, emotionless eyes.

For a moment, Carey was absolutely paralysed. Something was happening – something dreadful – but he didn't know what. He wanted to scream but his voice refused to respond to the command of his will. His mind was dizzy. His body was numb.

Then, abruptly, the spell broken, it was over. He slumped low in his chair, nearly toppling to the floor. Turning away, Villion crossed the room and sat as before.

Villion said, 'Speak, Carey.'

'Speak, Carey,' said Carey, at exactly the same moment as Villion.

Hearing his own words, Carey again wanted to scream, but his voice was not his. Villion had spoken through Carey's lips.

'Yes,' said Villion. 'I'm afraid, Carey, you're going to have to get used to having a passenger in your brain. There's no need to be afraid. You can speak and act as you desire on most occasions, but when it's necessary, I'll be there to assume control.'

'This . . . is . . . monstrous,' said Carey.

Villion shrugged, showing his unconcern. 'Now go,' he said.

'Now go,' said Carey, simultaneously.

Involuntarily, he stumbled to his feet and, like a man in a trance, turned and headed for the door. His feet moved as if propelled by a will of their own. As he walked, he heard a voice laughing behind him. He wanted to turn to see who it was, but his feet refused to let him.

CHAPTER 5

Among the Dynarx

The Dynarx were not the first intelligent alien species confronted by the human race during its drive to occupy the Galaxy. More than a hundred separate races had preceded them, with the bulk of these rather easily gathered up into the general scheme of the Empire of Man; the Dynarx, however, were different. Put simply, the Dynarx were the first alien species to teach the human race a most valuable lesson: that the Galaxy was not, as some men had sometimes believed, a private human reserve.

At the time of their discovery by men, the Dynarx occupied a thousand planets. To the discoverers, these worlds represented untold riches, and the initial reports received on Earth concerning the Dynarx system were filled with excited superlatives that barely concealed the greed of the men who made them.

Unfortunately, after filing these reports and announcing their intention to establish personal contact with the dominant aliens of the region, the discoverers were never heard from again. They vanished as swiftly and utterly as though they had never existed.

The initial reports of such alien wealth naturally inspired others to follow, but these men, and their ships as well, vanished as completely as the first. Expedition followed expedition into the great Sargasso Sea of the Dynarx realm. None was ever heard from again.

The Empire took notice. Initial puzzlement turned to rage, and a great fleet of four hundred warships was launched against the Dynarx. These warships reached their destination and then promptly vanished. No sign was ever found of any of them again.

After this, the anger turned to fear.

Meetings were convened in the imperial palace. Alternatives were discussed. In the end, the Emperor – a greedy but not a foolish man – did the only wise thing. He issued a proclamation declaring the entire sphere of Dynarx occupation outside the bounds of human expansion. The Galaxy was a big place, he reasoned. One thousand planets more or less . . . well, that still gave the human race several billion others to fill.

In the centuries since the issue of the imperial proclamation, a few brave men had chosen to ignore the decree and visit the Dynarx in spite of it. Some of these men later returned but most did not. The imperial authorities pretended not to notice. They had other problems with which to deal. By this time, the Empire of Man was engaged in a centuries-long war with another advanced alien species, the Wykzl.

Wilson, the renegade robot, was the most recent individual to visit the Dynarx. He, of course, had returned.

He had an explanation, too. 'It's a question of motive,' he told Tedric, as their ship plummeted towards the pale blue world which, according to Wilson, housed the bulk of the Dynarx population. 'The first explorers wanted to steal. The fleet wanted to kill and destroy. Me, all I wanted was knowledge. You tell me. If you were the Dynarx, wouldn't you have responded differently to different stimuli?'

'Perhaps,' said Tedric, 'but that still doesn't explain what happened to all those men who disappeared. No one ever reported sighting an enemy fleet. What sort of weapons do the Dynarx possess?'

Wilson shook his head and grinned. 'I doubt that they've ever developed a gun.'

'Then how?'

'When you meet them, you'll find out,' Wilson said. 'When I left the Dynarx, I promised to keep their secrets to myself.' He turned to Captain Juvi Jerome and winked. 'Surely you people don't object to an old outlaw keeping his promises, do you?'

Captain Jerome told him coldly that she personally did

not mind. During the voyage, Wilson had been paying her a sort of special courtly attention that she did not especially appreciate. Juvi was the first woman to serve in the Imperial Corps in many centuries and she felt she had proven her ability to stand on her own when she had helped save Tedric's life aboard the Iron Sphere. Besides, Wilson's attentions seemed to make Yod Cartwright jealous, and that was an additional complication she did not need in her life right now.

With the others, Juvi turned and watched on the view-screen as the strange planet grew in size. When the ship landed, she disembarked, her boot heels digging deep holes in the soft blue sand as she, Tedric, and Wilson moved across the flat, empty terrain. Tedric had ordered Ky-shan to remain aboard ship. The Wykzl and Dynarx were ancient enemies who could not bear the sight of one another. Yod Cartwright – to his considerable frustration – had been delegated by Tedric to keep the alien company. For herself, Juvi felt more relaxed temporarily freed from the strain of constant tension between Yod and Wilson.

Abruptly, the robot halted and pointed across the blue desert. 'Here they come,' he said. 'Let's wait for them.'

Juvi looked across the flat sandy ground and studied the alien creatures who were quickly approaching. She had, of course, never seen a Dynarx before. They were always described as resembling green slugs, but now, as she watched, Juvi decided that wasn't entirely fair. The Dynarx were by no means repulsive in appearance. More than slugs, they reminded Juvi of frolicking dolphins. The Dynarx seemed to bounce across the land rather than slide over it. They had several small flippers on their bottoms that appeared to propel them, bright pink eyes, and broad toothless mouths frozen in perpetual smiles.

It didn't take her long to decide, based on first impressions, that she liked these aliens.

You are a pretty one too.

The thought entered her mind from without. Startled, she swung her head. 'What did . . . ?'

38

'Hush,' said Wilson, who was beside her. 'Let them come closer.'

The Dynarx continued their steady approach and stopped a few yards from the three of them. There were nine of the aliens. After a momentary pause, one moved away from the others, and bounced up close to Wilson, who leaned forward and patted the alien on top of its head. His lips moved, but Wilson did not speak aloud.

Two more Dynarx broke from the group, one approaching Tedric and the other Juvi. She bent forward as Wilson had done and patted the alien's head. The flesh was warm and smooth to the touch.

You are a kind, clean entity.

Again, the thought just popped into her head. She stared. 'Did . . . did you speak to me?' she asked aloud.

We speak. I am Dynarx.

She turned her head and saw Wilson watching. 'That's right,' he said. 'They're telepathic. But don't worry. They won't peek at your innermost secrets unless they're invited.'

Tedric was listening, too. 'Mine said it was Dynarx. Not *a* Dynarx, just Dynarx. What does that mean?'

'It means they're all the same,' Wilson said.

'I don't understand,' said Juvi. 'Mine said the same thing.'

'I don't claim to understand it either,' Wilson said, 'but I know it's a fact. The Dynarx have separate bodies, enough to occupy a thousand planets, but there's only a single vast mind. When one speaks to you, they all do.'

'Was that the secret?' she said.

'It's a pretty good one, isn't it?' he said, with a grin.

The Dynarx had all turned around, their snouts pointing across the bleak land away from the ship. *You follow us*, said a voice in her head. She looked at Tedric and Wilson and guessed they had received the same message.

Tedric took a small communicator from the pocket of his silver suit and spoke into it. 'Ky-shan, this is Tedric. We've established contact with the Dynarx.'

'Yes, I see on the screen,' said the Wykzl's tight, disembodied voice.

'They've invited us to follow them. I think we'd better go.'

'I hope it is not treachery, Lord Tedric.'

'They seem peaceful enough, Ky-shan.'

'If you believe so.' The voice sounded disappointed.

'I'll keep in contact.'

'Yes, Tedric.'

'Damned prejudiced fool,' said Wilson.

Tedric pocketed the communicator. 'I hope you're right,' he told Wilson.

They moved forward, following in the wake of their Dynarx escort. The walk proved a lengthy one, and the ship soon vanished from sight over the horizon. The land remained as desolate as before. Finally, Juvi spied a large patch of green in the unbroken blueness ahead. She told Wilson and Tedric.

The robot nodded thoughtfully. 'Then that ought to be them,' he said.

When they drew closer, Juvi saw what Wilson meant. The patch of green was shown to be a gathering of Dynarx, hundreds of them at least. At the edge of the Dynarx stood a single, small, flat-roofed cabin. Juvi couldn't figure it out. Where had the wood come from to build such a structure?

Wilson nodded happily when he saw the cabin. 'That's where I stayed when I was here the other time. They've brought it back for me.'

Tedric seemed no less puzzled than Juvi but, since he said nothing, she also remained silent. Their escort left them in front of the cabin and merged into the mass of Dynarx. Wilson sat down in the sand. 'Well,' he said, 'how much of it have you figured out?'

'You mean there's more,' she said. 'It's not just telepathy.'

'No, much more. Think about it. What do we have here? A species sufficiently advanced to ward off the whole human race and yet one those capital city – and that's what this is, believe me – doesn't have a single building. You tell me the secret.'

She shook her head. 'I don't know,' she admitted. 'Does there have to be one?'

'Tedric?' said Wilson.

'You'll have to explain it to me, too.' He seemed oddly distracted, as though his thoughts were far away.

'Then you admit it doesn't make sense?' said Wilson.

Juvi nodded while Tedric remained motionless. 'Yes,' she said.

'How would you like it if the Dynarx built a real city?'

'I don't see how they could. Not in this wilderness.'

'Then watch. I'll get you one. Just give me a moment.' Wilson shut his eyes and leaned against the cabin wall. His breathing slowed and his whole body stiffened. He could have been in a complete trance, but then she noticed that his lips were moving. Puzzled even more than ever, she started to speak but Tedric laid a soft hand on her arm.

'Not now. Let him do what he wants. We can ask questions later.'

It happened without warning. One moment, the land around them was a vast blue desert. The next moment, a city stood on the sand. Only a few feet from the cabin a five-hundred-foot glass, steel and concrete building soared towards the sky. It wasn't the only one. Everywhere she looked, buildings as tall – or even taller – swept into the air.

'Bless the Lords of the Universe,' she said softly.

Wilson opened his eyes and grinned. 'See? I told you I'd get you a city.'

'You did this?'

'Well . . .' He laughed. 'No, I'm afraid it wasn't me. Credit the Dynarx. I asked for a city and they gave me one.'

'Oh, then it's not real.'

'It's as real as anything else in this universe. Watch.' Striding over to the base of the nearest building, he gave the wall a kick. They could hear the solid smack of his boot striking the concrete. 'And look up there,' he said, pointing.

She looked where he was pointing. It took her a moment to see what he meant, but then she spotted the faces pressed to the windows. As high as she could see, faces and more faces. Smiling faces. Dynarx faces.

The Dynarx had occupied their new city.

'Any more questions?' Wilson said smugly.

'Just one,' she said. 'How did they do it?'

He shrugged. 'I haven't the slightest idea. All I know is that they can do it and they do do it. You talked about reality. I think that's the key. For the Dynarx, there's no such thing as a single, set reality. Anything that can exist, does exist. They pick and choose, shifting from reality to reality. Right now, out of consideration for us, reality is this city. It doesn't have to be. It can be the big blue desert we saw before or it can be anything else. There were times when I was here before when . . . well, you would have had to have been here to understand. Maybe you will – later.'

She continued to stare at the city. 'It's like magic,' she said.

'And maybe that's what it is,' he said, 'though I honestly doubt it. After all, to a savage, our ship would seem like magic. To us, this is.'

Wilson moved towards the building. He waved. 'Come on. Let's find a place to hang our hats.'

Tedric again seemed distracted but he followed Wilson and so did Juvi. They found a set of glass doors and stepped through into a lush lobby decorated with various kinetic action paintings. Wilson marched to the elevator and called it down. The building appeared to contain apartments, like many such buildings in New Melbourne or other major Earth metropolises. Juvi hesitated before boarding the elevator. Chuckling, Wilson pulled her inside. 'It's real,' he said. 'I promise you.'

He punched the button for the seventeenth floor.

'Why there?' she asked, as the elevator rose with the three of them inside.

'It's where our apartment is located.'

'How do you know?'

'Because I have a certain fondness for the number seventeen and asked the Dynarx to put us there.'

In the seventeenth floor corridor, they passed a number of open doors. Curious, Juvi glanced inside and saw several Dynarx in each apartment, moving comfortably about as though they had lived there all their lives. Wilson led them to the end of the corridor and opened a door.

Inside was a large, well-furnished, six-room apartment. Juvi walked slowly through it, marvelling at what she found. Even the food cupboards were well stocked.

'I couldn't actually eat this, could I?' she said, holding up a ripe red tomato.

'I don't see why not,' said Wilson.

'I mean, if I did, I couldn't live on it. Magic is magic, but you can't grow tomatoes in a desert.'

'The Dynarx can. I lived on their food for years when I was here before.'

She shook her head and took a tentative bite. The tomato was sweet and full of juice. 'Magic,' she said, taking another bite, 'but good.'

She went over to the window and gazed out at the city spread below. The tall buildings such as this one occupied only a relatively small space at the centre of the city, but various smaller houses stood for miles around. This city wasn't nearly as large as New Melbourne, which covered the entire continent of Australia, but it seemed no less real, at least not from up here. She could see a smokestack puffing darkly and there was a big iron bridge with a green river running swiftly beneath it.

'I hope the Dynarx don't decide to switch realities all of a sudden. I wouldn't want to have this building disappear with us standing in the middle of it.'

Wilson laughed. 'The Dynarx are always considerate of others. At least as long as you're considerate back at them. If you're not . . . well, you can see what they're capable of.'

She nodded. That last sentence had given her a chill. She was beginning to comprehend how the great Imperial space fleet had been made to vanish. After all, if the Dynarx could wish a city into existence, they could also wish a fleet into non-existence.

Tedric stood in the middle of the main room, a tight strained look on his face. He had made no attempt to investigate the apartment further and had not spoken since they'd entered the building.

'We came here for a purpose,' he said, turning impatiently to Wilson. 'Maybe it's time we got on with it.'

'Is something wrong?' Wilson said, clearly puzzled by Tedric's abruptness.

Tedric nodded. 'Yes. For one thing, Fra Villion knows we're here.'

'But how could . . . ?'

'Never mind.' Tedric shook his head. 'This *vemplar*. I came here to see him. Where is he now?'

'Pal Galmain?' Wilson shrugged. 'I suppose he ought to be somewhere on the planet. I'll ask the Dynarx to . . .'

'Do it,' said Tedric. 'And now. Wherever he is, have him brought here as soon as possible. We seem to have much less time than I originally imagined.'

'I wouldn't worry about Fra Villion,' Wilson said. 'He can't harm us here.'

'I'm more concerned with us harming him than him harming us.'

Tedric's impatience puzzled Juvi. To tell the truth, she had forgotten all about their real reason for being here during the excitement of the past few moments. But Tedric came from another sphere of reality – Commander Nolan had told her that long ago – and to him everything in this universe must seem like a marvel. What they had witnessed today was no more or less fantastic than a spaceship or even a motor car. Tedric was the savage Wilson had used for an example.

'All right,' Wilson said. 'I'll find your *vemplar* for you if you're really that worried.'

He sat down on the carpeted floor, shut his eyes, and went into another trance. The minutes dragged by slowly, as Tedric and Juvi watched in silence.

Suddenly, in one corner of the room, a flash of motion

caught her eye. Turning, she nearly screamed. Fra Villion was staring back at her.

Wilson came suddenly to his feet. 'Pal Galmain,' he said, hurrying across his room. 'Am I pleased to see you again!'

The creature who looked exactly like Fra Villion put out one huge hand and clasped Wilson firmly by the wrist.

'And I am pleased to see you as well, friend Wilson,' he said.

CHAPTER 6

Pal Galmain

The creature who had materialised in the apartment on the Dynarx planet was not, of course, Fra Villion, and in fact, as a closer inspection revealed, any physical resemblance between the two was purely superficial.

But Pal Galmain was a Bioman – and a *vemplar*. He stood close to seven feet off the floor. Black fur covered the parts of his body – hands and throat – left exposed by the black cape and jumpsuit he wore. His face was hairless and the skin was a deep blue shade.

Wilson performed the necessary introductions. Galmain's sudden arrival had apparently caught even him by surprise. The *vemplar* nodded coldly at Tedric but, when introduced to Juvi, he first stared intently, then smiled – showing a row of white sparkling teeth – and bowed deeply at the waist. Taking her fingers in his, he bent down and kissed her hand. 'A most rare and extreme privilege,' he said in a soft melodious voice like the purr of a cat. 'You are most beautiful.'

Juvi failed to conceal her embarrassment and delight. Her face flushed red and she smiled happily. Tedric was grateful for his decision to leave Yod Cartwright behind in the ship. If the boy was jealous of Wilson, what would he be feeling now?

Glancing at Wilson and Juvi, Tedric decided it might be wisest to talk to Galmain alone, without the distraction of an audience. Wilson understood this, too. Catching Juvi by the wrist, he pulled her towards the door. 'Let's go out and look at the gardens,' he suggested.

'But there aren't any gardens,' she said, swinging her head to peer at Pal Galmain.

'By the time we get there, there will be,' Wilson replied.

When Tedric and Galmain were alone, the two of them stood motionless for a long moment trying to size one another up, like duelists waiting for the signal to begin. It was Pal Galmain who first broke the silence.

'So you are the mighty Lord Tedric of the Marshes.' His voice contained more than a touch of sarcasm.

'And you are one of the wondrous black knights of the Biomen,' said Tedric in a matching tone that served to conceal his surprise at Galmain's form of address. His full title was something Tedric seldom used in this universe.

'I believe we have a certain acquaintance in common,' Galmain said.

Tedric nodded. 'I assume you mean Fra Villion.'

'Yes. In spite of my exiled state, I do make an attempt to keep abreast of current events. Especially those involving Fra Villion.'

'Are you aware of his present whereabouts?'

'He has recently returned to Tavera and your arrival here did not greatly surprise me: Am I to assume you intend to proceed further?'

'I do. To Tavera itself, if necessary. Wilson told me about you. He suggested you might be willing to provide information and assistance. He said you held no love for Fra Villion.'

'That is true but . . .' The *vemplar* shrugged one massive shoulder. 'Villion and I share the blood oath. I may despise him personally, but I am no friend of your Empire of Man either.'

'I believe that Villion is a danger to much more than the Empire.'

Galmain showed a spark of interest. 'Perhaps you should elucidate.'

Tedric did. As quickly as possible, he described the details of Villion's recent ventures in the Empire of Man. Much of this would have been known to Pal Galmain, but some of it might not be. Tedric placed particular emphasis on Villion's assault on the Earth, his use of the Iron Sphere and the matter-scrambler.

Galmain smiled grimly. 'Villion's use of the Iron Sphere did create some controversy on Tavera, I believe. The vessel was an ancient device, originally built to withstand an outside attack. Villion took the Iron Sphere without permission. Its subsequent loss was a considerable blow to his prestige. Still, his standing among the *vemplars* proved sufficient to see him through the crisis. Villion possesses a glib tongue and a powerful force of will. Many of my colleagues, alas, appear to have neither.'

Tedric sensed the depth of Galmain's bitterness at his exile. It was, he realised, something that might be turned to his own advantage.

'But you have still failed to explain,' Galmain went on, 'why Villion represents a threat to more than your own race.'

'Because of whom I believe he serves.'

'And who is that?'

'Are you familiar with the red clouds?'

Galmain nodded carefully. His face was without any expression, but Tedric knew he had the *vemplar* interested now. 'I am aware of the existence of such phenomena, yes.'

'I understand that at least one cloud has appeared within the Bioman Sphere.'

'In an outlying region, yes. The cloud does not at present offer a cause for alarm. Still, it represents a danger that must be dealt with in time. I believe some measures have already been taken towards that end.'

'What sort of measures?' Tedric asked, excited by the thought that the Biomen had discovered a means for combating the clouds.

Galmain smiled. 'Unsuccessful measures, I'm afraid.'

'In that case,' said Tedric, 'it might interest you to know that Fra Villion is in the service of whatever it is that's behind the existence of the clouds.'

Galmain's expression became even more grim. He showed no sign of surprise at Tedric's revelation. 'The darker forces,' he said musingly.

'Who?' asked Tedric, sensing a slip on the *vemplar*'s part.

Pal Galmain shook his head. 'Never mind. What proof do you have to support this claim?'

'The fact that Villion both entered and fled the Empire by way of one of the clouds. The fact also that the Scientists have told me in confidence that this is the case.'

'The Scientists?' Galmain sounded genuinely impressed. 'You are in contact with them?'

'I serve them.'

'Then that explains much. Not only about you – but about Fra Villion. What you have told me only confirms certain conjectures of my own. During my stay in this realm, I have had much time for thought and speculation. I long ago came to fear that Villion might be in the service of those whom you claim.'

'But you can't tell me any more about the nature of these beings – who they are, where they originate, their purpose in attacking the Galaxy?'

'I'm afraid I cannot. So far as I am aware, no one can answer your questions except, presumably, Fra Villion. Their presence in the Galaxy is not recent. The *vemplar* archives, which I consulted before my exile, contain numerous past references to their existence. My own acquaintance dates back perhaps a decade of your years. At that time I was approached – telepathically – and offered employment. The voice in my mind did not identify itself, but I'm now certain it was indeed one of these beings. I refused the offer immediately. Few details were revealed, but what little I learned from the voice disturbed me deeply. I said nothing of the offer to anyone else. The ancient code of the *vemplars* forbids one knight to discuss with another the terms of his employment. I erred in interpreting the code too strictly. Apparently, later on, Villion was similarly approached. It would now seem that unlike me he did not refuse the offer.'

'Do I gather you believe there's a connection between your refusal, Villion's acceptance and your present exile?'

Pal Galmain nodded. 'From what you have told me, I am now certain of it.' His eyes blazed with sudden fury. 'Fra

Villion accused me of violating the ancient code by accepting an offer of employment designed to harm the Biomen as a whole. I could not understand how he even knew of the offer. I defended myself but his evidence consisted of lies and distortions. I was convicted and sent into exile. Until now, I have assumed Villion's motives were personal. I was a powerful knight and he was ambitious. I have underestimated the depth of his treachery. The offer I refused is the one he accepted.'

Tedric decided to attempt to take advantage of Galmain's anger. 'In that case, would you be willing to assist me? If we can defeat Villion, it might be possible to force him to admit his deceit. You could then return to your own home.'

Galmain shook his head wearily. 'It is too late for that, I am afraid. Although I may not look it, I am very old and not well. The desire to return to Tavera has long since withered within me. I expect to die here – and soon.'

Tedric thought quickly. Galmain's assistance was essential to the success of his mission. To attempt to enter the Bioman Sphere alone bordered on the suicidal. With Galmain's aid, the odds against failure would surely rise. 'The fate of the universe may be at stake. I am not exaggerating. The forces Villion serves are intent upon cosmic destruction.'

Galmain remained silent for a long moment. 'It will be very dangerous – with me or without me.'

'I expect that.'

'And perhaps impossible.'

'It has to be tried.'

'There is no greater warrior in the Galaxy than Fra Villion.'

'I have locked swords with him in the past and survived.'

'That was in your own realm. This will be his.'

'It must be done,' Tedric said flatly.

'All right.' Galmain sighed. He peered at Tedric, then nodded. 'If you are willing, then so am I. There may be a way. What you have told me constitutes a most serious charge against Fra Villion. If I were to violate the terms of my exile to return to Tavera to present this charge, I do not believe I would be refused entry. You and your crew could accompany me as witnesses. Once on Tavera, however, I can guarantee little. The case against Villion, even if it is heard, will surely be dismissed. At the very least I will be required to return here. As for your fate, I can promise nothing.'

'But what about the case?' said Tedric. 'Why are you certain it will fail? It's true, isn't it? When I told you, you believed me. Why shouldn't the others – the jury . . . whatever you use – why shouldn't they do the same? I can prove everything I said about Villion and the clouds.'

'I believed you because I was sympathetic but all you can prove is that Villion entered one of the clouds. When you think about it, to an unbiased observer, that really means nothing. Villion will simply claim that he was conducting a personal evaluation of the nature of the clouds. As far as what the Scientists told you, only they can confirm the truth of that, and I doubt that they would be willing to come to Tavera to testify against Villion.'

'No,' said Tedric, who was well aware of the Scientists' reluctance to intervene in human affairs.

'Then I can promise you no more than I already have: a chance to reach Tavera. After that, what transpires will be of your own making and responsibility.'

'I understand,' Tedric said. To be truthful, what Pal Galmain was offering was far more than he had expected. Face to face with Villion, Tedric firmly believed he could and would prevail. He put out his hand. 'Would you like to seal the agreement?'

Galmain hesitated for a long moment. Then one hairy hand shot out from his side. Tedric and the Bioman shook firmly.

Pal Galmain withdrew his hand and stared at the palm. 'I don't believe I have ever touched a mere human being before.' He looked up at Tedric and smiled gently. For the first time even his eyes seemed amused. 'But perhaps I am underestimating you.'

Tedric shook his head. 'I am only a man, Pal Galmain.'

'Perhaps. But you are also either a great fool or a mighty

warrior. No one else would dare face Fra Villion with the equanimity you have shown.'

'I don't believe I am a fool,' said Tedric.

Galmain nodded. He no longer looked amused. 'I hope for both our sakes you are right.'

CHAPTER 7

Into the Bioman Sphere

As a Bioman *vemplar*, Pal Galmain was little aware of the small pleasures of life. Of the larger forms of delight – of love, for example – he was as lacking in knowledge as any robot. And yet if Wilson, the renegade robot, was not a typical example of his breed, Pal Galmain was quickly learning that he was no longer typical of his either.

At one time, to be sure, he had been. Even now, as in his conversation with Tedric, he tried to give the impression that nothing had changed. But that was a lie – and he knew it. Pal Galmain had lived among the Dynarx and, after that, nothing could ever be the same for him. What he had seen and learned and experienced during the years he had spent among those green, slug-like aliens had shown him more truth of the fragile nature of cosmic reality than all his centuries among his own kind ever had. It was because of this – because of what he had learned among the Dynarx – that he had now fallen in love.

The only significant differences between Biomen and normal human beings were psychological. The mental senses that in most human beings lay dormant throughout their lives were put to use by the Biomen as easily and naturally as their eyes or ears or fingertips. Any adult Bioman could move his body through space, change his appearance, or communicate his thoughts over interstellar distances at will.

Still, physically and inwardly, Biomen remained human beings. Despite their bold attempt to convince others to think otherwise, Biomen were subject to all the normal human frailties, including hunger, disease, old age and death.

The Bioman race, like the human race, was also divided into two sexes, male and female. These two groups interrelated, sometimes formed permanent relationships, occasionally produced children, but never fell in love.

As a *vemplar*, Pal Galmain had had little contact with females, who as a group were never admitted into the ranks of the black knights. It was an omission – if indeed it was an omission – that he had barely noticed.

Since the Dynarx had long since passed beyond the need for separate sexes, the first female of any kind Pal Galmain had seen since his exile from Tavera was Captain Juvi Jerome of the Imperial Corps. As naturally as a raindrop dropping from a cloud, the *vemplar* had fallen instantly and irrevocably in love with her.

It didn't make sense. But that was the primary lesson Pal Galmain had learned from the Dynarx – that existence need not make sense, that cause and effect was an illusion – so he tried not to be disturbed. His initial reaction was simply to ignore the emotion. Since it was strange and unfamiliar, he pretended that it did not exist.

He failed. As long as he remained close to Juvi Jerome, his love for her did not lessen. He loved her with all of his heart and soul; he knew he could never bear to be parted from her for long.

During the course of his conversation with Tedric in the apartment, there had never really been any doubt that he would in the end agree to assist the humans in their mission against Fra Villion. It wasn't hatred that motivated him. The truth was that he had long since forgotten to hate even Villion. It was love.

So now, in the small ship, as it slipped past the invisible boundary that divided the realm of the Dynarx from the Bioman Sphere, Pal Galmain sat talking with Juvi Jerome. They were alone in the ship's cockpit. It was her watch, but he had slipped quietly away from the others in the larger bunkroom in the rear to join her. The viewscreens showed the utter blankness of N-space. A console calendar announced that the ship would be re-entering normal space in the vicinity of Tavera in fifty-two hours, seventeen minutes, nine seconds.

54

'So even though you weren't born a *vemplar*,' said Juvi, 'you really can't remember what it was like not to be one.'

They were discussing his past. It was a subject he had never spoken about with anyone before, but with Juvi it seemed almost inescapable. He didn't really understand why. Obviously, it had something to do with falling in love.

'Those who are destined to be admitted to the ranks of the knights,' he said, 'are chosen by lottery at birth, and those selected are immediately subjected to rigorous physical, mental, and psychological exams. Those who fail are destroyed – painlessly. It is my understanding that barely one in ten lottery winners do survive.'

'How horrible,' she said.

He nodded. Before the Dynarx he would never have done that, but now, even though he wasn't sure he agreed with her remark, he at least understood why she made it.

'But I was one of those who passed. I was taken immediately to Tavera and placed in Sanctuary, a huge stone castle that's the only building on the whole planet. From the earliest time I can remember, I was learning what it meant to be a *vemplar*. Combat training began when I was six. At thirteen, I fought my first duel. At twenty, I recited the blood oath of the ancient code.'

'What's that?'

He shook his head. 'If I could tell you, I would, but I'm afraid it's not possible.'

'Is it a secret?'

'No,' he said, 'but it's very complicated. It took me twenty of your Earth years to learn the code and nine months to recite it. Ignoring the complexities, the code requires every *vemplar* to remain loyal to the group, the species and himself – in that order. Failure to observe any tenet of the code, no matter how obscure, is punishable by death or, as in my case, permanent exile.'

'I thought Fra Villion lied to have you sent away.'

'He did.' He spoke sadly but without bitterness. 'Villion, of course, wanted me dead, but because of my centuries of service among the *vemplars*, I was offered the traditional choice of exile. I could either die by my own hand or else go and live anywhere in the Galaxy so long as I never again entered the Bioman Sphere. To Fra Villion's immense displeasure, I elected the second alternative. Life was somehow important to me then. I suppose I believed I needed it in order to have my revenge upon Villion.'

'But you went to the Dynarx.'

'I did. No *vemplar* had chosen exile within the memory of the eldest knight. It was difficult for me to decide where to turn. The Wykzl would have killed me. You humans would have spurned me. That left either the Dynarx or isolation. I chose the Dynarx, but I'm not really sure why. Perhaps my luck – all *vemplars* believe devoutly in luck – had suddenly altered for the good.'

'Then you were happy among them?'

'I wouldn't say that, no. I was happy as a *vemplar*, but then I was blind. Please remember that. If you hope to defeat Villion, you must understand the weakness he shares with me.'

'How is he blind?'

'He fails to see the things the Dynarx taught me. He is blind to the truth of death and life. Since the Dynarx never die, they are the only experts on the subject.'

She looked puzzled. 'Wilson told me something about that. He said the Dynarx have a drug. If they swallow it, they die, but in a few hours they wake up and live again. I don't understand it, but he says it works.'

'It does. I took that drug.'

She nodded, apparently impressed. 'But was it real? I mean, you didn't actually die, did you?'

'As far as I know, I did, and since I think I did, what else matters?'

'Can you tell me what it was like to die?'

He smiled wistfully. 'I can't. Words are not part of the universe of death. It's a translation problem, a totally different language.'

'You make it sound terribly frightening.'

'No, it's not that. Death is many, many things, but it's

56

never really frightening. I wish it had been possible for you to remain among the Dynarx long enough to undergo the experience. If you had, then you would understand why I cannot describe it. If I had my way, it would be mandatory for all intelligent living things to die at least once in their lives.'

She laughed. 'That just proves you're still a *vemplar* at heart. You don't want to let even death be a matter of choice.'

Her derision wounded him, even though he knew she did not mean to be hurtful. He said, 'Perhaps you're right. I may not have been born a *vemplar*, but undoubtedly I will die one.'

She patted his hand. 'I don't think that's so dreadful.'

Her touch was like electricity. 'No?'

'I think you're fine the way you are. Maybe that's odd. I certainly didn't care much for what I saw of Fra Villion.'

He was finally able to laugh, too. 'No one cares much for Fra Villion.'

'Except Lola Dass.'

'Who's that?'

'The human woman who was with Villion aboard the Iron Sphere. Her husband was the man who invented the matter-scrambler. He was a kind man, if a little crazy, and when she left him and went to Villion, it made him even crazier. That was lucky for us, for Tedric and Yod and me, because then he tried to kill Villion by destroying the Sphere. He succeeded and saved the Earth, but Villion and Lola managed to escape, and Milton Dass was the one who died. I don't think he minded. By then, his own life wasn't as important to him as destroying Villion.'

Pal Galmain nodded thoughtfully. Tedric had told him some of this, but not about the woman. The concept was a difficult one to grasp: Villion and a woman. What could it mean? 'Is Fra Villion in love with her?' he asked.

Juvi shook her head immediately. 'No. Lola Dass is very beautiful. Even I have to admit she's the loveliest woman I've ever known. I think Fra Villion just collected her – like

57

a trophy. She belonged to someone else. She was a prize to be taken.'

Juvi's knowledge of human – and Bioman – behaviour impressed him. Few *vemplars* could fathom the intricacies of another's mind; it was not something they had been trained to do. 'Does she love him?'

Juvi smiled. 'If you'd met Lola Dass, you wouldn't have to ask. Villion was a trophy for her, too. The only person Lola loves is herself.'

'She's like a *vemplar* in that,' he said.

'Which is probably what makes her and Villion such a good team.'

'I see.' He stared morosely into space, his mood suddenly troubled, although he wasn't entirely sure why. Perhaps it was partly due to the way she had pointed out to him, in spite of all that had transpired during his years among the Dynarx, that he was still basically a *vemplar*, a black knight. Under the skin, where it truly counted, he and Fra Villion were like brothers; their parents – the heritage that had molded them – was the same. Understanding this made him understand something else: he was not as free from the motive of revenge as he liked to think. If and when the final showdown came it would be he, Pal Galmain, who would rise to face Fra Villion. The moment of conflict was inevitable. He felt little satisfaction. Now that the moment he had been seeking had nearly come, he was forced to contemplate the reality of facing Villion. If he met Villion and failed to defeat him, he would die, but if he won, he would also die, albeit in a different, less physical way. As the conqueror of Villion, he would surely be forced to resume his former life on Tavera, and that, after the Dynarx, was the same as death.

'Pal Galmain,' said Juvi.

He looked up. 'Yes?'

'I was wondering about your appearance, the way you look. Is it true that you Biomen can alter your features at will?'

'Yes, we can.'

'How?'

58

'It's relatively simple for us, no harder than it is for you to paint your lips.'

Blushing slightly, she reached up and touched her red mouth. 'It's a habit I fell into.'

He stroked the fur at his neck. 'Maybe that's all this is too – a habit. Would you like to see me without it?'

'As you really are?'

'Let's say as I really should be. What do you think?'

'Well . . .' She considered. 'Well, yes. I think I would. I mean, if you don't object. It's just the resemblance to Fra Villion. That's what bothers me.'

'Then shut your eyes.'

'Can't I watch?'

'I want it to be a surprise.'

'All right.' She shut her eyes tightly. 'Go ahead.'

He did. The analogy he had used was actually less than accurate: for a Bioman, altering appearance was no more difficult than blinking an eye. Within a matter of seconds, Pal Galmain was done.

'You can look.'

She opened her eyes and stared. Her expression registered surprise, then wonder, then delight. 'You look just like a man – a handsome man.'

'Why, thank you,' he said, nodding with dignity. He meant what he said. It had been such a long time since he'd last worn his natural face that he barely recalled what it looked like but, since she was pleased, so was he.

Reaching into the rear pocket of her silver uniform, Juvi extracted a square object that glittered in the overhead light. 'Look in here,' she said, extending the mirror out towards him.

He took it in his hand and peered at the glass. The face that stared back at him was so ordinary in appearance – so human – that he found it difficult to realise it was only himself. A square jaw. Shallow cheeks and a strong nose. Deep blue eyes. Thin lips. His complexion was a pale shade of pink. Looking up at Juvi, he forced a smile. 'I don't know if I'd use the word handsome.'

'You're modest. See how young you look. You could pass for thirty.'

'Biomen never do look old. Not until they die.'

'Now you're just being morbid.'

'It's easy to do – under the circumstances. I haven't been on such close terms with myself in centuries.'

She smiled, though he hadn't meant to be funny. 'You can change back if you want. I've had my wish. I'll close my eyes again.'

'I thought you liked it.'

'I do.'

'Then I'll keep it.'

'Really?'

He nodded. 'Sure.'

She laughed. 'Boy, are you going to surprise the others. They'll think we have a stowaway on board.'

'Don't worry about them. What about poor Fra Villion? He won't know what to think. All these years he's been copying me. When I turn up looking like this, he won't know what to do.'

She was laughing with him when, suddenly, she stopped, turned, and hurried across the room. Galmain stared after her and then his ears also picked up the noise she had heard. In the console across the room, a warning alarm was sounding shrilly.

'What is it?' he asked, following her, the question of his appearance now forgotten.

'There's a ship out there.' She pointed to the large viewscreen. 'I think it's approaching us.'

He could see nothing on the screen except, perhaps, in the middle of the vast grey emptiness of N-space, a small silver speck. But the instruments spoke clearly enough for one who knew their language.

'Can you tell whose?' he asked.

She shook her head. 'Not yet, but I don't think it's an Imperial ship. Not way out here.'

'It wouldn't be Wykzl either,' he said. 'And the Dynarx rarely travel through N-space. That leaves only the Biomen.'

'The same thing had occurred to me.'

He raised his eyes and looked at the viewscreen again. The silver speck had grown. It was clearly a ship, but still not close enough for a definite outline to be discernible.

'You'd better alert Tedric,' he said.

'Yes.' She turned without another word and hurried towards the rear.

Alone, Pal Galmain glanced from the instruments to the viewscreen and back again. As the ship continued to grow in size, he became more convinced of the accuracy of his initial supposition. The ship was not only a Bioman ship, but he was nearly as certain of its exact origin. The high velocity the ship was maintaining was almost clear proof that it came from Tavera; it was a *vemplar* ship.

He heard footsteps behind and looked back. Tedric stopped in his tracks and stared in amazement. Pal Galmain grinned and tried to explain, but Juvi beat him to it.

'Pal Galmain has decided to change back to his normal face,' she said, with what sounded almost like pride.

Tedric nodded, glanced at Galmain another time, then shrugged his big shoulders. He came forward and looked up at the screen. 'Is it one of yours?' he asked Galmain.

'I believe it is. A *vemplar* attack-cruiser more than likely. It'll be heavily armed and three times as fast as this tug.'

'You expect it to attack?' Tedric said.

'I doubt that it's intercepted our path by accident. If I were you, I'd order everyone to battle stations immediately.'

'I agree.' Turning, Tedric gave Juvi the order. She scurried away to deliver it. Tedric turned back to Pal Galmain. 'I don't suppose I could ask you to help.'

'You don't need to ask. I'm volunteering.'

'They are your people.'

'If this ship burns with me in it, that's not going to mean much, is it?'

'Then handle the shields. I'll steer.'

'Fine,' said Pal Galmain. He glanced at the viewscreen once more, then crossed the room to assume his station.

CHAPTER 8

Skirmish and Capture

Under normal circumstances, a small spacetug such as the one occupied by Tedric and his crew would not have been armed for battle. Prior to his departure from Earth, however, Tedric had taken the precaution of having this particular tug equipped with a forceshield and heatrays.

Now, in the grey depths of N-space somewhere between the realm of the Dynarx and the Bioman Sphere, Tedric's foresight was about to be justified.

The tug's limited firepower was packed into four heatray turrets, one located at each end of the cigar-shaped hull and two more on the sides. A single forceshield could be activated from the cockpit to protect the entire ship from enemy fire, but in order for the turrets to return that fire the shield would have to be temporarily lowered. Neither the shield nor the heatrays were especially strong or powerful. Tedric, entering the alien Bioman Sphere, had not wished to offer too threatening a presence. Whether that decision represented an error in tactics would not be determined for certain until the approaching ship closed, attacked, and displayed the full range of its own armaments.

As he lay nestled in the lower gun turret, Yod Cartwright thought of all these things and regarded them with care. There was a bitter, acrid taste on the back of his tongue and he realised with some annoyance that it might be fear. Yod kept one eye tightly fastened to the round tube of the gun sight that protruded from the instrument panel in front of him. Through the sight he could observe the enemy ship, magnified several times over, as it drew closer. It's no bigger than we are, he thought with some optimism, but he knew that size was no way of measuring its strength. If it was a warship, no matter how large, the chances were good it was easily capable of blowing the tug clear into another universe.

The gun sight suddenly flashed red. The colour showed only for a split second, but it would not have been possible to miss it. Yod understood the meaning of the signal. It meant that the forceshield had been activated. If the light flashed again – though blue this time – it would mean that the shield had been temporarily lowered and the turret gunners, including himself, should be prepared to fire their rays. He knew, when that light came, he would have to be quick. The shield would remain down for no more than a few seconds before another red light flashed and it was reactivated. After that, if he mistakenly fired an additional bolt, the ray would strike the interior of the shield and rebound back . . . with fatal consequences.

Yod wore a set of earphones strapped to his head, but the tug's communication system remained silent. Yod sympath- ised. He didn't particularly feel like talking. The taste in his mouth had grown more sour. He kept trying to swallow, but his throat refused to work properly.

Darkness surrounded him here in the turret, but with one eye fixed to the gun sight and the other squeezed shut for better vision, he had little chance to be aware of it. In the sight, the bulk of the enemy ship loomed even larger. He could see the forward turret, a black wart of lead extending from the rounded silver cone of the ship's snout. More than likely there was a man nestled in that turret. A man like me, Yod thought, except that he's a Bioman who wants to kill me.

Two blue beams, straight as parallel lines, shot out from the sides of the ship. Yod felt the tug jerk under him as the beams caught hold. He knew what they were: tractor beams, lines of magnetised energy designed to catch and hold an enemy ship. In the Imperial navy, tractor beams were normally only found aboard the big battlecruisers with sufficient energy reserves to operate them. It was a bad sign for a small ship such as this to possess tractor beams in its arsenal.

Yod felt the hull buck gently around him and then, suddenly, through the gun sight, he saw the enemy ship turn an apparent somersault. His own stomach did a funny flipflop in response and by the time he had recovered, the ship was already a long way off, its tractor beams waving impotently in the void.

Tedric, at the tug controls, had managed to break free from the tractor beams. Because of the ease with which that manoeuvre had been accomplished, Yod assumed the beams could not have been especially strong. He decided to count that as a very good sign indeed.

'We might try to hit them now.' The voice in the earphones was soft, and Yod recognised Wilson speaking from the forward turret. 'We could try a stern pass.'

Yod had been as surprised as anyone when Wilson had decided not to remain on the Dynarx planet. It had been his understanding that Wilson would not accompany them farther, but the robot had explained that he had an urge for one more bout of adventure in his life before retiring for good. Tedric had welcomed Wilson's continued presence. Yod had not. He was sure Wilson was after Juvi Jerome and that his intentions were less than honourable. Yod came from Drexon's World, a planet notorious throughout the Empire of Man for its rigidly puritanical code of behaviour. Juvi was constantly laughing at him because of his beliefs, but in this instance he thought she was the one who was being naive. Wilson wasn't only interested in the keenness of her mind. On several occasions Yod had tried to warn Juvi about this but she insisted he was only being jealous, a charge that was, as far as he was concerned, utterly ridiculous.

In spite of his gnawing thoughts, Yod kept his eye firmly fixed on the gun sight and the enemy ship. The tractor beams had now been withdrawn, and the ship was following a course at an angle to the tug, drawing steadily closer. Yod pressed his thumb snugly against the trigger mechanism, knowing the moment of combat could not now be far distant. With his other hand he turned a small wheel on the side of the gun sight tube, increasing the magnification of the lens. He focused on the ship's forward gun turret, the target Tedric had assigned him. The enemy ship was undoubtedly protected by a defensive forceshield in the same way as the tug. It would be Yod's task, once the firing began, to try to penetrate that shield.

'We'll let them fire first,' said Tedric's confident voice over the radio, cutting smoothly through the gathering tension. 'There's no reason not to be polite about this.'

'What about them?' Juvi said. She was in the upper gun turret and sounded only slightly less assured than Tedric. 'Is there any chance they might be peaceful?'

'It doesn't look good. I tried to call them with no success. They raised their shield before we did.' Radio waves could no more penetrate a forceshield than a heatray could. Their conversations would be private.

'How shall we fire?' asked Wilson from his position in the forward turret. 'A broadside? Or should we try to pinpoint?'

'We'll try to pinpoint first,' said Tedric. 'If he manoeuvres better than us and we can't hold him, we'll have to switch to a broadside and hope for the best.'

Yod nodded silently, concurring with Tedric's choice of tactics. A broadside was really only effective when one ship outgunned the other by a considerable degree and could afford to try to wear down its opponent. Pinpoint firing did require superior manoeuvrability, but when a ship had it, it was the best and fastest way of penetrating an enemy shield. Yod didn't know a great deal about the tactics of deep space warfare, even though he had watched numerous tridee serials as a boy, but what Tedric said seemed to make sense. He was beginning to feel slightly more confident himself. The bitter taste in his mouth didn't go away, but he noticed it less.

The sudden burst of yellow light erupting from the enemy ship caught him by surprise. He fell back and his eye jerked away from the gun sight as the tug gave an abrupt lurch and seemed to dive. Grabbing for the gun sight, he pressed his eye against the lens, but he had lost his fix and saw nothing but N-space. He reduced the magnification and searched wildly for the enemy ship. The tug pitched and rolled, zigged and zagged, as Tedric manoeuvred to keep their shield as free as possible of enemy fire. Occasional excited voices crackled in his ears, but Yod didn't bother trying to listen. The bitter taste in his mouth had vanished. He was tense but clearheaded. Forcing his hand to remain steady, he continued to try to find his target again.

There it was. The enemy ship streaked through the void. Oddly, all of its firepower seemed concentrated in the forward gun turret, burst following burst at split-second intervals, while the other gun stations remained dark. Keeping the ship in view, Yod increased the magnification and moved in closer. The bursts of yellow light emanating from the turret distracted him and he blinked to keep his vision from blurring. Infrequently, one burst splashed more broadly than the others, and Yod knew that the shield had been hit.

'We're holding up well,' said the cool voice of the *vemplar*, Pal Galmain. 'We're outmanoeuvring him. He's missing more often than he's hitting.'

'I'm going to try to get on top of him,' Tedric said.

'Be cautious,' Galmain said. 'He's only using one turret. It could be a trick.'

'If things get hot, we'll beat a rapid retreat. Grab hold of your seats. Here we go.'

Giving a sudden lurch, the tug seemed to vault straight upwards. Since the enemy ship was the only point of reference in the void, it seemed to descend simultaneously until the tug hung neatly suspended above it. Tedric kept to a zigzag course even here, and the enemy heatray bursts struck home less than one time in ten.

'It's been thirty seconds since he opened fire,' said Tedric, shocking Yod, for whom it had seemed more like thirty hours. 'He can't keep it up much longer. He's going to have to reload.'

Through the gun sight, Yod could see that the forward turret was still the only one firing. With the tug hanging directly above the ship, he could think of no reason for the ship to attempt to conceal its firepower; it had already lured the tug in as close as it ever possibly could. Yod was beginning to feel a great deal more confident. They were going to win, damn it, they really were. This was starting to be almost fun.

Tedric seemed to have the same idea. 'Yod, Juvi, Wilson, I want you to focus your fire on that forward turret. Ky-shan, I'm afraid you'll have to aim somewhere at the middle. See if you can poke a hole through the hull. We'll hit him from this angle. I'll put us into a roll. Yod and Juvi, that way you'll be able to fire in tandem. As soon as his shield goes up, be ready. We've got to hit him quick and hard. I don't think we have sufficient energy resources for more than a ten or fifteen second barrage.'

Yod felt that he was ready. His thumb lay touching the trigger mechanism – almost too tightly. Without warning, the gun sight suddenly flashed blue. The enemy had ceased firing and raised their forceshield.

At the same instant, Tedric must have lowered their own.

Yod fired his first bolt. Tedric threw the tug into a gentle roll. As the enemy ship spun out of view, Yod kept his eye fixed to the gun sight. When he could see it again, he fired a second bolt. The flashes of yellow light, now that he knew they were his own, seemed even more brilliant than before. He blinked his eyes continuously to keep his vision clear. When he wasn't firing, Juvi was. Wilson, from his strategic position in the front, was able to maintain a steady stream of heatray fire. Yod could see the effects of Ky-shan's rear gun, too. The hull near the middle of the ship gleamed a dull red. That meant the shield had been penetrated there.

The enemy ship did nothing to evade their assault. It maintained its straight, unswerving course. Yod knew that every one of his bolts must be striking home and so undoubtedly were the others. They were not only winning the battle, it was fast becoming a rout.

Then the gun sight flared red. Immediately, Yod let go of the trigger and tried to relax. The ship righted itself and ceased spinning. It was only then, with the enemy ship directly underneath him, that Yod could survey the damage they had inflicted. The forceshield must have been penetrated almost at once, for the whole front end of the ship was nothing more than a blob of melted, twisted metal. A big jagged hole, Ky-shan's work, gaped in the middle of the hull. It seemed to go clear through the ship and out the bottom side.

'I think his shield's permanently gone,' Tedric said softly. 'There's no reason to hit him any more.'

The cheering in his ears, mostly from Wilson and Juvi, sounded a little hollow even to Yod. Their victory had come too easily. Nonetheless, he couldn't help himself. He joined in the celebration.

'Shall we board her?' asked Wilson, his old pirating instincts reasserting themselves.

'I think we should try,' Tedric said. 'I'll put our lock against that hole in the middle. Maintain battle stations until we do.'

Yod peered through the gun sight as Tedric manoeuvred the tug close to the wounded ship. When the two hulls touched and locked, cutting off any chance of a last desperate assault, he turned, opened the turret door, and crawled out. Juvi was already descending the ladder above.

'We beat them,' she said with a broad grin.

'You sound like you weren't sure all along.'

'I wasn't. I've always heard these Biomen were supposed to be supermen.'

'Then you must have heard it from Pal Galmain.'

He spoke in an undertone but one loud enough for her to hear. Politely, she pretended she hadn't. In the cockpit, the two of them found Tedric, Wilson, and Galmain waiting. Ky-shan joined them a few moments later. Tedric was wearing a bulky, air-tight vacuum suit, the bubble helmet tucked under an arm. He motioned to Yod and Juvi. 'You two will come with me. We're going to check out our prize.'

Yod found a pair of vacuum suits in a wall locker and handed one to Juvi. He snuggled inside his suit, then helped

Juvi with her helmet. She helped him. He took a deep breath, activating the suit's oxygen valve, and exhaled comfortably. He signalled to Tedric, who had also put his helmet on, that he was ready.

'How about the radio?' said Tedric's voice in his helmet.

'Mine's fine,' said Yod. He heard Juvi say the same.

'Got your guns?'

Yod and Juvi had both kept their heatguns free. Yod clutched his in his gloved hand.

'Then let's go.' Tedric led the way into the airlock. 'I have no idea what we'll find,' he said as they waited for the outer door to open. 'Pal Galmain seems to think the whole thing may still be a trap, but I can't see any reason for it. Still, we ought to be careful.'

The door opened. They found themselves standing in front of the big hole Ky-shan's heatray had torn in the ship's hull. It was necessary to re-orientate their sense of direction since the hole was in the Bioman ship's roof. There was also a second hole – in the floor of the ship – but it was a smaller one. The greyness of N-space showed through.

'Let's jump for the floor,' said Tedric.

He leaped first. Yod followed. It was more like jumping ahead than down, but the ship's grav-systems were still functioning, and when he hit the floor he stayed there on his hands and knees not far from the smaller hole. He slid slightly aside and a moment later Juvi landed beside him.

Yod looked around. They had landed in an enclosed cabin, the contents of which, whatever they might once have been, were now a mass of ash and rubble. There were steel doors at both ends of the cabin.

His heatgun extended in front of him, Tedric approached one of the doors. He burned a hole through the lock and kicked the door open.

The room on the opposite side had not been badly damaged. The wall panelling had been largely ripped out for some reason but a thick carpet and several big pillows covered the floor.

A suited figure lounged on one of the pillows.

As the three of them cautiously entered the cabin, their guns extended, the figure stood, holding its hands over its head. The figure was of normal height and looked like a man.

'Don't shoot,' said a voice over the radio. 'I surrender.'

Yod thought he recognised the voice. He wasn't sure, though, until Tedric exclaimed: 'Carey!'

'Why, Tedric, old friend,' said Matthew Carey, former Emperor of Man. He lumbered forward, his hands still extended above his helmeted head. 'Fancy running into you in a place like this.'

CHAPTER 9

A New Threat

After completing his inspection of the Bioman ship and finding no one else aboard, Tedric took Matthew Carey back to the tug and introduced him to Wilson and Pal Galmain. Carey's eyes bulged with surprise when he learned the identity of the *vemplar*, but he volunteered nothing until Tedric sat him down beside the control panel console and said, 'All right, Carey, how about an explanation?'

On the surface, Carey seemed as calm and at ease as ever, but there was a certain tenseness in the way he spoke that puzzled Tedric. Carey grinned and said, 'First of all, I want to thank you for having saved my life just now.'

'I wasn't aware that we had,' said Tedric. The other members of the crew formed a curious half-circle around Carey. The two ships remained locked together in their firm embrace.

'Of course you did,' said Carey. 'Why do you think Fra Villion put me on that ship?'

'I was hoping you'd tell us that. Why did Villion send you here? What were you doing with him?'

'Well, as you probably know, Villion escaped from the Iron Sphere and I must tell you how pleased I was about that. I may have been under his spell for a time – he's a powerful personality – but I'm still a human being at heart, and I didn't want to see the Earth I love wiped out by that mad fiend.'

Tedric withheld comment. He had been aboard the Iron Sphere in the days preceding Villion's assault on Earth, and if Carey had in any way objected to his mentor's plan of attack, Tedric had seen no evidence to indicate it. 'Why don't you just tell us about Fra Villion?' he prodded.

'All right, I will. I just didn't want you to misjudge me.'

'I'm sure I haven't,' Tedric said drily.

Carey nodded and went on: 'Well, when he escaped, Villion forced me to accompany him. I didn't want to go – I was willing to surrender to Nolan and accept my just punishment – but Villion is a difficult man to resist. He worked some spell on my mind. I lost consciousness and when I awoke I was already in the Bioman Sphere.'

'You remember nothing of your passage there?'

Carey shook his head. 'No.'

'Nothing of the red cloud?'

'The cloud? How does . . . ?'

'Villion apparently left the Empire by way of the red cloud.'

'I remember nothing of that,' said Carey. 'I was aboard the Iron Sphere. The next thing I knew, I was in the Bioman Sphere.'

'Where is the Sphere exactly?' asked Pal Galmain. His eyes were cold and his manner suspicious.

'A planet called Tavera. It's an ugly place, the head-quarters, I believe, of all the *vemplars*. I was kept in a castle known as Sanctuary, a most unpleasant place. The entire planet is, for that matter. It's one vast cold desert. I can't understand why anyone in his right mind would choose to live there willingly.'

'There are other aspects to life,' said Pal Galmain, 'than easy comforts. But tell me, was Villion at Sanctuary too?'

'Oh, yes. In fact, he seemed to be running the show. Not that I knew very much of what was going on. I was kept locked up in my room. Villion wouldn't even see me. I was beginning to think I'd die in that hell.'

'You appear to have come this far,' Galmain said tightly, 'alive.'

Carey's face beamed a smile, as if he were oblivious to the *vemplar's* hostility. 'That was Villion's idea, not mine. I don't know why you're all here or what you're after, though I suppose I could make a good guess if I wanted, but Villion knows about it too. He called me to his room one day and told me he was sending me into space to meet Tedric. At

72

first I was delighted – I thought I might be rescued – but when I found out what he really intended, I was shocked. He'd equipped a robot ship to come here and attack you and he wanted me along for the ride.'

'Why?' asked Galmain bluntly. Tedric leaned back and let the *vemplar* take control of the interrogation. Galmain was clearly sceptical of Carey's tale, and Tedric believed that was a wise viewpoint to hold.

'He wanted me dead,' Carey said. 'That's the only thing I can assume. I guess he'd finally realised I wasn't going to help him any more. The way I see it, he thought either you'd destroy the robot ship – and me with it – or else the ship would destroy you, in which case he'd still lose nothing. If you want the truth, I doubt if the ship was even programmed to return home. I think I would have been marooned in N-space forever. Now you can understand why I say you saved my life.'

'But you came as Villion directed,' Galmain said. 'You're here.'

'Do you think that was my idea?' For the first time, Carey's voice carried a trace of real passion. 'I told Villion to send one of his own people. I pleaded with him. He said I was the most expendable individual on Tavera. He laughed when he said that, and I realised by then how much he'd come to despise me.'

'Villion would never despise a mere human being,' Pal Galmain said. 'He wouldn't expend the effort.'

Carey shrugged. 'All I know is the way he acted towards me.'

'But how could Villion be certain that what actually transpired would not occur, that you would survive and fall into our hands?'

'That was my doing,' Carey said, with a clear note of pride. 'I disengaged the gun turrets, all except the one up front which I couldn't reach.'

'And Villion let you do that?' Galmain frowned deeply. 'He is not that great a fool.'

'I never said he was. He locked me in a cabin. Tedric can

confirm that – he had to burn a hole through the door to reach me. What Villion forgot, though, was that I know a good deal about the circuitry of robot ships. I studied for two years at the Corps Academy on Nexus. Tedric can tell you. The subject is pretty well covered there.'

Tedric nodded. 'That's true enough. Carey would know about such ships.'

'Enough to realise that any circuitry connecting the main controls with the gun turrets would have to pass through the walls of my cabin. I simply took the panelling apart until I found what I was looking for. Then I tore out the wires with my bare hands. I had to be careful. I didn't want to cut off my own heat or air or gravity.'

Tedric nodded thoughtfully. 'He's telling the truth about that at least. The panelling in his room had been removed.'

'And could have been removed even before he left Tavera,' said Pal Galmain.

'Why would I want to do that?' Carey said.

'You didn't. Fra Villion did.'

'But why?'

'To place you among us. To lull our suspicions. To make you a spy.'

'But if that was true, then why didn't Villion disconnect all the gun turrets? He could have put me in a different cabin – up front – and used the same story. After all, that one turret might well have been enough to destroy you. If that had happened, then what?'

'If that one turret had not functioned, your plan would never have succeeded.'

'I don't understand,' Carey said.

'Nor do I,' said Tedric.

'It's quite simple. If the robot ship had failed to open fire on us, we would have gone past. After all, were we seeking a battle? No. If the robot ship hadn't given us one, we would not have stopped and found this spy to take into our midst.'

Carey looked bemused. 'I never thought of that.'

'No,' said Galmain, 'but I'm sure Fra Villion did.'

To his credit, Carey did not attempt to appear more

innocent than he actually was. He fastened his gaze on Tedric and said, 'I'm telling the truth. I can't force you to believe me, but, damn it, this time I am.' As he spoke, that peculiar rigidity came over his voice again. Tedric wished he knew what it meant.

'I, for one, do not believe you,' Pal Galmain said. He faced Tedric. 'My recommendation is that we dispose of this spy forthwith. Put him back aboard the robot ship, make certain the controls are properly destroyed, and set him adrift. If what you have told me of his past activities is true, it's a just fate.'

Carey looked stunned, but it was Juvi who spoke: 'That's horrible, Pal Galmain.'

'Execution is never pleasant, Juvi, only necessary. The man is not merely a spy, he's worse: a traitor to his own kind.'

'But I can help you,' Carey said imploringly. 'I know what you're after. You want Villion. Well, I know how you can reach him.'

'Your assistance won't be necessary, I'm sure,' Pal Galmain said. 'I have visited Tavera before. I can locate the planet without help.'

'And Villion will blow you out of the sky before you ever land. He's not about to let you get close to him.'

'I have certain charges to bring against Villion. According to the blood oath of the ancient code . . .'

Carey laughed. 'The only blood involved in this is going to be yours.'

Tedric intervened gently. 'What is it you have in mind, Carey?'

'Simply this. What will Villion be worried about? Your ship, that's what. If the other one returns, the robot ship, mine, he's not going to know what to think. He'll have to let it land so that he can investigate.'

'You're suggesting we change ships,' Tedric said.

'Exactly. I don't think the control systems have been damaged. It'll take some work, some time, to do it right, but I'm positive something can be rigged up.'

'And we'll be totally disarmed,' said Galmain.

'What chance do you think you stand now, this tug against an entire planet?'

Tedric looked at the *vemplar*. 'What he says does make sense, Pal Galmain.'

'Then we'll do it,' Galmain said, 'but that's no reason to spare Carey. We can leave him aboard this ship and set it adrift.'

'You're acting like a bloodthirsty maniac,' Juvi said. 'Why are you so eager to kill this man?'

'Because it's the only logical course to pursue,' said Galmain.

Tedric realised it was time to settle the matter of Carey's fate. He looked at the *vemplar*. 'I suspect your appraisal of the situation is valid, Pal Galmain,' he said, 'but I don't happen to believe that mere suspicion is sufficient grounds for taking Carey's life. His suggestion, we all agree, is an excellent one. Therefore, we will change ships. I'm not prepared to trust Carey fully – not at this time at least. He will be locked in a cabin and kept there for the duration of our voyage.'

'It's still a risk,' Galmain said. 'An unnecessary one.'

'I don't dispute that it's a risk,' said Tedric. 'Whether it's necessary is a different question, the answer to which depends upon the value one places on a human life.' Tedric stepped away from the group, went to a vacant chair and sat down heavily. 'There's one other matter, something I haven't told any of you so far. I think the time has come for you – all of you, including Carey – to be aware of this. Just after our arrival in the Dynarx realm, a Scientist, Skandos, contacted me. He informed me that a new red cloud had recently appeared within the boundaries of the Empire of Man. This cloud, unlike the previous one, is not located in an uninhabited, isolated sector of the Empire. It is huddled just outside the orbit of Pluto and is presently expanding at a very rapid rate. Already, the forces described by the Wykzl are affecting the population of Earth. There has been a great panic and madness runs rampant. Within a few months – a local year at the most – the cloud will swallow up the Earth and its sun. Evacuation procedures have been instituted, but because of the general state of chaos, it is doubtful that more than a small percentage of the Earth's inhabitants can be removed in time.'

His announcement was greeted with hushed silence. Even Carey looked stunned.

'What can we do?' said Juvi.

'Only one thing: proceed with our mission. The red clouds are apparently the tools of what Pal Galmain calls the darker forces and what the Scientists know as their adversaries. The only contact we have with this group is through Fra Villion, their agent. For us to reach them, we must first reach Villion. Perhaps now you can understand my willingness to take risks. The situation is critical. If we fail, it will mean millions of lives.'

A hushed atmosphere prevailed. All eyes were fixed on Tedric as if expecting him to provide sudden enlightenment. The best he could manage for them was a defiant smile.

He came to his feet. 'So let's get on with it. To prepare our new home is going to require a lot of work. If we don't get started, we'll never get done.'

Pal Galmain nodded in agreement. 'Then it's on to Tavera. You for your reasons and I for mine.'

'For victory or death,' Yod Cartwright exclaimed dramatically.

'Or maybe both,' said Wilson, with a crooked smile and a wink for Juvi.

CHAPTER 10

Lady Alyc

Physically, Lady Alyc Carey was blind, but the handicap was one that she had long since accepted. While it might be said that for others – for strangers – she was without sight, for those that mattered – for herself and her friends – her vision was as keen and perceptive as if she could actually see. The fact that she was blind was no more significant than the fact that her skin was white. Blindness was not a handicap; it was merely a characteristic.

Alyc had last actually seen at the age of seven. As a child, the only daughter of Melor Carey, richest and most powerful man in the Galaxy, she had been pampered and adored by her father – her whims were his commands and her desires his goals. In her entire life until then, nothing had transpired to challenge her basic assumption that the universe had been created strictly as a plaything for herself.

In that year, the year when Alyc turned seven, the leading astronomers of the Empire announced that a certain obscure, planetless star, KC97Z, was about to explode into a nova. When Alyc heard of this, she expressed the wish to be present at the actual moment of the explosion. Melor Carey, as the richest and most powerful man in the Galaxy, promptly sought and obtained permission to visit the site. As the moment approached, the Carey family yacht, *Blue Eagle*, docked in the vicinity of KC97Z. There were a number of other ships present. Most contained scientists come to observe and study the nova.

Since astronomical phenomena were part of the universe, Alyc naturally assumed that this nova had been created for her own personal entertainment, so that, when the explosion occurred and everyone else – including her father and brother – observed the event by viewscreen, Alyc sneaked away and opened a sealed porthole and watched with her own naked eyes. She had been warned, but since the universe was her plaything, she could not imagine how it might in any way harm her.

She was wrong. When KC97Z exploded, Alyc Carey, for one infinitesimally brief moment, was witness to the raw unvarnished truth about the universe. She learned that it was not her plaything; rather, she was its toy. This instant of enlightenment was something Alyc never forgot. It was also when she was struck blind.

That was many years ago. Alyc had by now thoroughly reconciled herself to the fact that the universe was a cold, cruel environment that cared no more for her whims and desires than a boot heel cared for the bug it so casually squashed. This conclusion had made her a different person.

For many years of her blindness, Alyc had lived an isolated existence in the Carey family home on the Carey family planet, but that world – Milrod Eleven – had been destroyed by Milton Dass's matter-scrambler and Alyc had come to Earth to live. Recently, she had purchased a vast holding of land in what had once been known as the state of Colorado. It was springtime now as she stood on the rear platform of the small robo-flier and felt the cool afternoon breeze fluttering across her face.

A man stood beside her, observing the large herd of mustang horses grazing in the valley around them. As he watched, the man spoke to Alyc. 'I still say it makes no sense at all for you to stay here. There are millions who'd like to leave and cannot. You must be aware of the danger, even if you can't actually see it. I really don't understand. Why do you insist on staying?'

'I told you, Phillip,' she said. Her face was turned towards the herd. Although she could not see the horses, she could sense their near presence and was strangely soothed by it. 'I see no reason for me to leave Earth.'

'How much of a reason do you need?' said Phillip Nolan, in an exasperated voice. 'The red cloud is there. I'm not making it up. I've sent a dozen of my best corpsmen into the middle of it and none has come back. It's real, I'm telling you.'

She reached out and touched his hand reassuringly, gripping the fingers gently. 'I'm not doubting you, Phillip. I know it's there as you say. I can't see it, but neither can the wild horses, and they know too.'

'The horses . . .'

She nodded. 'See how restless they are. It didn't used to be that way. When Tedric was with me, he and I would come here every day. We would walk among the herd and they were not afraid, but now if I try to leave the flier, they run. It's not me they're afraid of. It's the cloud. It disturbs them.'

He shook his head. 'I'm not worried about those horses, Alyc, I'm worried about you.'

'It's the same with me,' she said flatly.

'Then you can feel it?'

'I can. It's like a scent in the air. A terrible, fearsome smell of evil.'

'I know what you mean. It's unbelievable what's been happening in New Melbourne. The whole city is like a mad-house. People burning, looting, killing – and for no reason. No one knows what to think. They're frightened and they don't know why. It's affected me too. In my dreams, I see things . . . even when I'm wide awake, I dream. It's the cloud. The Wykzl said it drove people mad. They were right. It's happening here – all over Earth. That's why you have to leave, Alyc. The Emperor has already gone and most of the court with him. I'm one of the few left and I'll be going soon, too. In a few weeks, the only people left on Earth will be the totally mad. You can't stay in a world like that.'

'You don't understand.' She released his hand and gestured at the landscape. In the far distance, the white gleaming peaks of the Rockies stood like fingers on the hands of a god. 'It's safe for me here. The mountains fear nothing.'

'But what about the people? You're not totally alone out here. When I flew in, I saw a settlement, a town . . .'

'An Indian village. They're strong people, like the mountains. They can endure anything – even the cloud.'

'I wouldn't want to place a bet on that. No, Alyc, it's just too dangerous. You have to leave Earth.'

'I left one home. That was enough. Tell me one thing, Phillip. What does the cloud look like?'

'I haven't seen it up close. Those who have say . . .'

'Not there. Here. What does it look like in the sky?'

'Well, you can only see it at night. It's like a brilliant band of fire cutting across the stars. It's awesome. And frightening. That's what I mean. You can't stay here another day. If I went away and left you, how could I ever face Tedric again?'

'Tedric will understand.'

'I'm not sure about that.'

'I am.'

'You act as if you've just finished talking to him.' He laughed uncomfortably.

'Not talked, no, but I've heard . . . I'm aware of his actions. Tedric is among friends. He knows of the cloud and is determined to save us.'

'He's reached the Bioman Sphere?'

'Yes.'

'But how do you know? Is it the Scientists? Have they contacted you?'

'In a manner of speaking, they have. Sometimes I hear them . . . talking. It began when I lost my sight. I hear voices, the Scientists – and others. Tedric will save us. If he fails, it will be because he is dead, and if he dies, then there's no need for me to go on living.'

'You shouldn't say that. Tedric wouldn't agree.'

'It's not Tedric's decision to make.' She turned away from him, sensing the lateness of the hour from the angle of the sun upon her face. 'Perhaps we should go. I know you have to return to New Melbourne.'

He nodded tightly and preceded her forwards into the

bubble cockpit. Nolan punched the control buttons and, as the flier rose into the air, turned in his seat and silently surveyed the flat, passionless land below. Alyc was also silent. Eventually, the ranch house appeared in front of them. There was a large garden in the back, a splash of rich colour amid the drab brown land.

When the flier landed, Nolan stepped out and helped Alyc to the ground. They stood in front of the house. Her robot gardener, Kuevee, stood motionlessly on the porch, a sprinkler can gripped in one hand.

'You can still change your mind,' he said. 'There's time. I'd gladly wait and help you pack.'

She shook her head. 'No, Phillip. My mind is made up.'

He sighed. 'You're no different from when you were a little girl. I remember you as the meanest, nastiest, most spoiled, most stubborn creature I'd ever met in my life.'

She smiled, knowing he meant no harm. 'Go, Phillip. I know you have work to do. You've wasted enough time on me.'

'Good-bye, Alyc.' He took her hand and, bending at the waist, pressed his lips against it.

'Good-bye, Phillip.'

'I still wish . . .'

'No,' she said firmly. 'You've done what you could. Now go.'

Reluctantly, he turned. A small, single-passenger rocket-plane stood on the ground nearby. Alyc waited until the harsh roar of the engines had dwindled to a tiny echo and then turned towards the house. 'You can put that silly can down now,' she told the robot, Kuevee. 'He's gone and I'm safe. Where is Kisha?'

'In the house, Alyc, preparing an evening feast.' The robot spoke in the clipped tones of its kind. Kuevee was an old-fashioned steel and aluminium machine programmed strictly for his gardening duties. In spite of this, Alyc thought he was more human than most of the people she'd ever met.

'You mean she's lurking in the kitchen with her nose

pressed to the window, trying to find out everything she can.'

With practised ease, Alyc climbed the steps, opened the front door and entered the house. The living room was spacious and warmly furnished. She found Kisha in the kitchen, busily engaged beside a woodburning stove. The subwoman looked up as Alyc entered the room.

'Ah, you're back.'

'As if you didn't know.'

Kisha shook her tiny feline head innocently. 'I've been busy – very busy.'

'I don't suppose you heard the rocketplane leave either.'

'What plane, Alyc?'

She laughed. 'Your protectiveness is overwhelming. You and Kuevee both. Phillip Nolan is an old, old friend. He would never harm me.'

'There's a madness in the air, Alyc. It is never wrong to be cautious.'

'Call me when dinner's ready, please. I'm going to rest first.'

Her feet never hesitating, she went up the stairs to her room. Poor Phillip, she thought, as she lay on the bed. What will become of him? If wasn't until today, out on the range, that she had realised for the first time that Phillip Nolan was in love with her. That could be a problem. Not a terrible problem. But a problem, nonetheless.

She shut her eyes and tried to relax, but as always lately, the fear – the great, nameless, reasonless fear – came over her. She began to shiver and shake. Tedric, she thought, hurry. Please hurry. You must or all of us are lost.

The Trial

The meeting hall in which the trial took place on the planet Prime at the edge of the Milky Way Galaxy was approximately the size of the continent of Australia. The ceiling was high, the floor of polished wood, and the walls ornately decorated. The defendant sat in a small chair to the right of the judge's tall desk, while the prosecutor stood to the far left, reading from a long parchment scroll. The jurors – four hundred strong – sat scattered in chairs throughout the room. From where he sat, the defendant could actually see no more than two or three of them, but he knew everyone was present and that all were listening attentively.

The defendant was Skandos, the histro-physicist, who stood accused of the crime of seeking to destroy the universe. The judge, Zorza, was the oldest and wisest of the Scientists, a man who had spoken only once before in ten thousand years. The prosecutor was Jorken, a relatively youthful Scientist – barely three thousand years of age. He was the one who had brought the charge against Skandos.

Jorken was presently reading from a lengthy description of Skandos's alleged crimes. The defendant sat with his chin resting on his palm, only partially aware of the events surrounding him. A larger part of his attention was focused on another set of events entirely. These were presently taking place many thousands of light-years away in a section of N-space between the realm of the Dynarx and the Bioman Sphere.

'. . . and so, in conclusion,' said Jorken, in his thin reedy voice, 'Skandos stands accused of the most heinous crimes imaginable. He has brought destruction and chaos to the very universe he pledged to protect and preserve. The evidence in support of these charges is unequivocal. As much as it grieves me, I must ask from you, his peers, the only conceivable verdict – guilty. A just punishment must then be imposed.'

Skandos nodded thoughtfully. He had a good idea what this punishment would be: exile. A punishment imposed only once in the history of Prime and then with most disastrous results. Not that it mattered. Skandos did not expect to be convicted or punished.

Sensing that Jorken had at last completed his recital, old Zorza leaned down from his high desk and peered at Skandos. 'How do you plead to these charges, my old friend?' he asked in a sad, gentle voice.

'I'm afraid,' Skandos said firmly, 'that I am guilty.' He waited for the murmur of astonishment to fade from his mind, then went on in a ringing voice. 'Guilty,' he said, 'of obedience to my pledge, of courage and perseverance in the face of a terrible challenge. It is possible that I may have erred. I admit that. It is possible that I may have been overly bold. I admit that, too. But I have committed no crime. Every action I have taken has been for the greater good of our universe as a whole, and I defy anyone' – he turned and glared at Jorken – 'to prove otherwise.'

'I'm afraid that's just what I've done,' said the prosecutor, with a smirk.

'Then you dispute Skandos's defence?' said Zorza.

'Of course I do.' Jorken's eyes blazed intensely. 'His defence is no defence at all. He has disputed none of the charges brought against him. The evidence stands as I initially gave it. The charges remain irrefutable.'

'In that you are wrong,' Skandos said softly.

'Would you be willing to put that claim to a test?'

'What do you have in mind?'

'These men are your friends. For obvious reasons, they are hesitant to pass judgment upon you. I'm asking only for you to permit yourself to be examined here by me today. Your defence appears to be that your motives were pure even if your deeds were not. I intend to prove, through the vehicle of your own words, that such a defence is utterly without relevance.'

Skandos shrugged. 'You may, if you wish, question me.'

Beaming eagerly, Jorken advanced on Skandos, his head cocked to one side, like a cat approaching its prey. 'Tell me, Skandos,' he said, 'are you acquainted with an individual known as Lord Tedric of the Marshes?'

'I am indeed,' Skandos said, in a strong, proud voice.

'And is it true that you chose to bring this individual into our universe in order to use him for purposes of your own?'

'I brought Tedric here solely through necessity. My calculations of historical probability had convinced me that our universe could not survive without his presence.'

'Then this Tedric is – how shall I put it? – he is our saviour?'

'He could be, yes.'

'And what sort of individual is this saviour? He is, I assume, some variety of super man?'

'Tedric is, in most respects, a normal human being, but he possesses certain . . .'

'He is, if I may interrupt, a barbarian, I do believe.'

Skandos frowned. 'That term has no real meaning. It is true that the universe from which Tedric came is not as outwardly civilised as ours. Nonetheless, in the time he has been with us, Tedric has managed to adapt himself to . . .'

'He has defied our adversaries. Is that correct?'

Skandos nodded firmly. 'It is why I brought him here, yes.'

Jorken turned with a triumphant smile and faced the largely invisible audience scattered through the vast meeting hall. 'I submit that Skandos has just convicted himself out of his own mouth. He admits he brought a barbarian into our universe and instructed him to defy our adversaries. The result of this massive intervention on the part of Skandos is apparent to all. The Earth – our ancient home planet – now faces utter extinction. Millions of lives will almost certainly be lost. And why? Because Skandos and his barbarian, through their intervention, forced our adversaries to reply in kind. There is an old saying – let sleeping tigers sleep. If Skandos had only let well enough alone . . .'

Skandos rose to his feet. 'Jorken,' he said slowly, 'please forgive me. But you are a fool. A damned stupid and ignorant fool.'

Jorken turned, his face crimson. 'How dare you . . .?'

'If Tedric had not been present here, the red cloud that threatens Earth would have done so years before now. Tedric has already granted us much time. If let alone to grow and develop, he can give us much, much more. Salvation? I cannot promise you that. But with Tedric, there is hope at least. Without him, there is only absolute universal doom.'

Jorken laughed harshly. 'You have no proof . . .'

'Perhaps not.' Skandos's voice rose. He was addressing not only Jorken but the entire assembly of Scientists. 'My friends, listen to me and listen closely. I admit to one crime and one crime only. I have kept certain truths from you. Our adversaries are not, as Jorken intimates, soundly sleeping. Rather, they are more awake and alert than any of you has guessed. The seriousness of these charges lodged against me, arising as they do out of a profound and abysmal ignorance' – he glanced at Jorken and frowned tightly – 'has convinced me that the time has come to share what I know with you. I am a histro-physicist. The discipline is an arcane one, but you are all aware of its basic precepts. Through an intimate knowledge of past and present and the use of higher mathematics, I am able to predict the probability of future events. I can tell you this much. Prior to Tedric's arrival here, a 99·9 per cent probability existed that this universe would shortly cease to exist. With Tedric's presence, that probability has fallen to 87·8 per cent.'

'And where are these figures?' Jorken cried, hastening to lessen the impact of Skandos's revelation. 'If they exist, then bring them here and let us see.'

'Alas,' said Skandos, 'although I could indeed produce my figures, I am afraid they would mean little to most of you. Histro-physics is a discipline that takes many centuries to master.'

'Then what you have offered us is nothing more than a bald assertion,' said Jorken. 'We demand proof, Skandos, firm and unyielding proof.'

'Aren't you neglecting one factor?' Skandos asked quietly.

Jorken frowned and slowly shook his head. 'I think not, no.'

'The fact is, whether you can understand them or not, these figures do exist. For untold eons, we and our adversaries have lived side by side in a state of general equilibrium. If our adversaries have now chosen to violate this truce and move towards universal destruction, aren't you curious to know why?'

'I am not curious because I do not believe they have done so.'

Skandos looked sad. 'Even five years ago, the probability of universal destruction was nil. Suddenly, the figure rose to 99·9 per cent. I am only asking why.'

Zorza peered down impatiently from his tall desk. 'Skandos,' he said firmly, 'if you have something more to reveal, I believe you should do so now.'

Skandos sighed. 'You are correct, Zorza. I'm afraid I've been guilty of toying with poor Jorken here. All right, the truth is simply this. In recent times, our adversaries have added a new recruit to their ranks. It is this individual who has turned them towards their newly aggressive policy of universal doom. This individual is one known to all of us here. His name is Sarpedion.'

The gasp of astonishment that invaded his mind did not surprise Skandos. He knew the impact of what he had finally revealed. Even Zorza's eyes grew wide with amazement. 'No!' he cried aloud.

'Yes,' said Skandos gently. 'Sarpedion. One of our own number. A Scientist exiled from Prime for the crime of interference in the affairs of another universe. Sarpedion has joined our adversaries and is now intent upon a plan of vengeance not only against us but against this whole universe. And he will succeed. My calculations prove that much. With Sarpedion at their head, our adversaries are fully capable of destroying the universe.'

'Except for Tedric,' said Zorza.

Skandos nodded. 'Except for Tedric.' He glanced at Jorken, who for once seemed to have nothing to say. 'And, very possibly, even with his help.'

'I move for an immediate dismissal of all charges against Skandos,' said Zorza, his voice quaking.

The immediate wave of assent that engulfed his mind should have gratified Skandos, but the truth was that he was no longer listening. The momentary distraction of the trial now passed, his attention was once more fixed upon that portion of N-space between the Dynarx realm and the Bioman Sphere.

But Tedric was no longer there. In the interim, he had moved on. Skandos sought to track him down and did so at last.

The planet was known as Tavera.

CHAPTER 12

Sarpedion

In a room in the castle Sanctuary on the planet Tavera, Fra Villion, the Bioman *vemplar*, peered through the thick window glass at the stone courtyard below, where a group of his fellow knights moved briskly through the ritual of their daily weapons exercise. As Villion watched the thin whip-sword blades cutting through the air, he felt a deep welling of painful regret. Not so very long ago, he would have been part of that stately dance, feeling the keen vibration of the sword against his palm, experiencing the only real pleasure a warrior ever could feel, when he and his weapon became, if only for an instant, a fused and irresistible whole. He sighed heavily, realising how, when he had accepted his present employment, he had given up all that forever. He would never dance in the courtyard again. He would never wield a whipsword for pleasure alone. If his present endeavours failed, he would surely be dead, and if they succeeded, the universe itself would be doomed. He had nothing left to look forward to – nothing at all.

The insistent voice of the woman finally succeeded in penetrating his thoughts. Turning from the window, Villion faced her and tried to conceal his irritation. Dressed in a tight fitting jumpsuit and black cape, her blonde hair spilling to her shoulders, skin of throat and face as white as the hottest star, Lola Dass stood near the bedroom door. Her grey eyes flared fiercely with amused contempt.

'I asked if you cared to come with me,' she said archly.

'I – no.' He shook his head, momentarily confused. 'Where are you going, may I ask?'

'Nowhere. Out for a walk. As disgusting as this world is, it's more bearable than this damned castle.'

'If you go out, stay away from the knights. I don't want their exercises interrupted.'

She laughed. 'Do you think I have any interest in bothering your poor stupid knights? I've seen them jumping about before. I don't see the point of it.'

'The point,' he said, 'is self-discipline.'

'Which is boring. Like you. Like everything on this planet.'

He viewed her with utter loathing. When he'd first seen Lola Dass, she had seemed irresistibly appealing, but he now realised that it had simply been a matter of his own vanity. Lola Dass, a beautiful object, had belonged to another man. So Villion had taken steps to acquire her, as he might have obtained a priceless painting or valuable sculpture. That poor Milton Dass. He had never understood his good fortune in being rid of this woman.

'I'm really not going to stand for this much longer,' she told him, her hands on her hips, one foot slightly in front of the other. 'You'd better be aware of that, Fra Villion. Until I'm free of this miserable hell, I'll make your life as unbearable as my own. I can do it, too. I'm promising you. Carey's gone. Now I want to go too.'

He smiled in spite of himself. 'Where Carey has gone, I doubt that you'd care to follow.'

Her expression grew interested. 'Have you killed him?'

'Not exactly, no.'

'Then what?'

'Never mind.' He'd long ago ceased sharing his plans with her.

'Then I won't. But remember this. I want to get out of here. I don't care where I go. Send me to Kleato, your capital. I understand it's one huge city, like New Melbourne on Earth. I'd enjoy it there.'

'I've explained the situation to you before.' He was trying to be patient. The depths of Lola's malevolency should not be underestimated. Milton Dass had made that mistake and paid for it with his life. Villion could easily kill her as she stood, but to do so would be to violate the blood oath of the ancient code – a murder for selfish reasons – and although he had broken the code several times, he had done so only at the behest of his present masters. Approaching Lola, he laid a furry hand upon the sleek skin of her neck. 'As soon as Tedric is destroyed, we will both go to Kleato. I promise you. It's a mere matter of days – hours.'

'Tedric,' she said with a bitter twist to her lips, sliding free of his grasp. 'Don't you know how sick to death I am of hearing that name? What is there about this Tedric that makes him so important? I've seen the man. He's a savage – an animal.'

'But a warrior,' said Villion softly. 'And a powerful one.'

She laughed. 'Powerful enough to have got the better of you in a duel, as I recall.'

Villion nodded, remembering too. Aboard the Iron Sphere, armed only with an unfamiliar whipsword, Tedric had indeed defeated him in open combat. Only Lola's unsolicited assistance and Tedric's own odd hesitance to kill had avoided a total disaster.

'But I don't really care what you do,' she said, moving at last to depart. 'You can kill Tedric or he can kill you. What does it matter? Who knows, if you're right about him, I might be better off with Tedric than with you.'

She slammed the door as she went out. Villion saw no need to reply to her final taunt. Tedric was too wise ever to ally himself with someone such as Lola. No matter who lived or died, her fate was firmly sealed to that of Fra Villion.

Villion felt a sudden tingling sensation in his head. For a long moment, crossing to the window and peering out, he pretended not to be aware of the signal. The tingling grew more insistent. His master was calling him, Villion knew, and he must answer. At last, stepping back, he shut his eyes and forced his mind to concentrate. He envisioned another room in the castle, one he knew well by now. A few seconds later, his body vanished from the bedroom. In an instant, it reappeared in the room he had pictured in his mind. It was a dark, dusty place, securely bolted from without.

'Sarpedion?' Villion called softly. 'Sarpedion, what do you want of me?'

He could sense the presence of a darker force. It bore neither shape nor mass. It was a thing – incorporeal, malignant, and real.

A voice invaded his mind: *Your agent has failed. Tedric has locked him away. You will learn no more from him.*

Villion shook his head. He had long ago learned the futility of trying to deceive this thing that seemed capable of reading his innermost throughts. 'Carey has performed his proper function. I now know Tedric's general intent. He will be coming here – to Tavera. When he arrives, I will be prepared to greet him.'

Are you so certain of success? said the voice, tauntingly.

'There are risks,' Villion admitted. 'My position among the knights is less secure than it once was. Reports of my activities in the Empire of Man have aroused some suspicions. I did not anticipate Pal Galmain's return. If his presence aboard Tedric's ship was discovered, our cause would be sorely wounded.'

Then you must strike before his presence is made known.

'That is my intent,' Villion said stiffly. 'The moment the ship enters normal space, a squadron of pursuit craft will rush to the attack. Tedric's ship lacks a functioning force-shield. My agent, Carey, saw to that.'

A wise manoeuvre, said the voice. *But a dangerous one as well. Surely, your colleagues will recognise the ship as one of their own.*

'I will invent a story that it was stolen by Carey. I will say that he assists an invasion force.'

For your sake, I hope the deceit proves sufficient. I sense that you fear this Pal Galmain.

'He is a powerful knight. In order to serve you, I had to drive him from Tavera. He has every reason to seek vengeance against me. But he is a mortal. He can be killed.'

Then do so.

Villion grew angry. 'You needn't state the obvious. Haven't I served you well? I have remained loyal to your cause while you have been less than honest with me. I was never told of the meaning of the red clouds. You never informed me of your overall goal in this universe. Do you think I would have agreed to serve you had I known the entire truth?'

As a matter of fact, Fra Villion, I do think so. Like all of your kind, you are utterly without so-called moral scruples. What does the death of this universe mean to you? Nothing. You will survive. I have promised you that.

'And why should I believe what you say?'

I neither know nor care what you choose to believe. Your miserable blood oath requires you to serve me or resign. Since you haven't resigned, I suggest we devote our attention to the matter at hand. The present situation is a critical one. Tedric must be killed and killed at once. To fail now is to guarantee your own ruin. Perhaps, if nothing else, you will believe me when I say that.

Villion nodded solemnly. 'I believe you, Sarpedion. And Tedric will die.'

Then go about your duties. We have no further need to speak. Once the act has been accomplished and Tedric lives no more, I shall return. When we speak next, the future will lie open to us like a rotting wound.

Those last ugly words ringing in his mind, Villion waited until he was sure the darker force had gone. Then he tried to take a deep breath, but the thick air in the enclosed room caught in his throat and he nearly gagged. Shutting his eyes, he desperately pictured his own bedroom. It seemed to take forever, but at last he felt his body jump through space.

Opening his eyes, he saw his own room around him. Lola had not returned. He sat down heavily on the bed and put his head in his hands. Finally, feeling his strength returning, he forced himself to stand and cross to the window. He looked out, but the knights were no longer there. The stone courtyard was empty and silent. A dim light filtered through the air. He must have spent hours with his master. Already, night was falling. Tomorrow, with the dawn, would come a new challenge to be met and won.

Villion stepped back and turned. Lola entered the room. When she saw him, she stopped and gave a little gasp of surprise. She knows, he thought without reason. She knows what I am and how much I have surrendered.

CHAPTER 13

Out of the Void

Even under the most favourable circumstances, the process of jumping a ship from N-space back into normal space could be a delicate operation. For Tedric, piloting a strange ship in an unfamiliar part of the Galaxy, it was a good deal more than that.

The ship's Bioman-built computer, an exceptionally sophisticated machine, now confirmed that it was within easy reach of its objective, the planet Tavera. Like anyone who had flown the spacelanes, however, Tedric was familiar with spacemen's tales of ships jumping from the void only to land smack inside a planet, moon, comet or star, and he hesitated. The reasons for such accidents were not clearly known. The captains of the ships involved had never survived to testify to their own possible miscalculations, and the gigantic explosions brought about by the phenomenon of two objects attempting to occupy the same space at the same time obliterated any trace of evidence. And so Tedric remained cautious. Perhaps excessively so. For more than an hour, the computer had proclaimed their ability to jump, but Tedric waited.

Wilson sat huddled in a small chair beside the computer station. That most ancient and proficient of all tools, a pencil, stuck out from the big fingers of one hand, and a sheet of hard tablet rested in the other. Catching Tedric's wandering gaze, Wilson nodded. 'I'm finished,' he said.

'What did you find?' Tedric asked.

'Exactly what I expected to find. I've double-checked every figure. The computer's right. We can jump.'

'Juvi?' said Tedric, turning slightly.

She sat close to Wilson. Tedric had given her the same task, checking the computer's figures. She glanced up from

96

her tablet and shook her head. 'I'll need another few minutes. I'm not a robot. This isn't easy for me.'

Tedric nodded, almost grateful for the additional delay. Everyone was present in the cockpit. Yod Cartwright stood near one wall, his gaze vague and dreamy, while Pal Galmain stood near another, his face remote and morose. Even Matthew Carey was here, released from his confinement. Carey occupied a chair close to the radio. Ky-shan stood over him, the giant blue-furred Wykzl serving as a guard.

Wilson, obviously impatient, drummed with his pencil. Tedric ignored the gesture. He was well aware of the true facts, that space was a vast empty waste and, even jumping blind, the chances of materialising inside any substantial object were slim. His reluctance to act was motivated by something more than mere timidity. It was a feeling he had.

Such feelings were nothing new. Ever since Skandos had first brought him to this universe, Tedric had experienced certain similarly restless moments of doubt. Skandos had long ago assured him that these feelings were indeed real and not the result of Scientists' tampering. Tedric still did not fully understand what the feelings meant. It wasn't so much that he was seeing the future but rather that he felt as though the present was something he had experienced before and that, as a result, he really ought to know what was coming next. But he never did. The future was as much a blank to him as to anyone. But he was worried. Something was wrong – something somewhere. He just didn't know what.

Juvi's voice broke into his thoughts. 'Tedric,' she said, laying her tablet aside, 'I'm done. My figures check, too.'

He nodded. 'All right.' A decision had been made. No matter how he felt, it was time to act. 'We're going to jump. Stations, everyone.'

Tedric moved over and sat in front of the ship's controls. He placed one hand on the wheel and the other on the throttle, oddly antique terms for devices that bore little resemblance to their original namesakes except in basic function. Juvi remained at the computer, while Wilson went over and sat close to the radio. Pal Galmain swept briskly across the room until he stood directly beneath the view-screen. Carey and Ky-shan remained as they were.

'Be ready,' Tedric told Juvi, who would be the one to actually order the computer to launch the jump. 'I'm going to place us into freefall now.'

'Aye, aye, sir,' she said, reverting to the old terminology as the moment drew near.

Tedric touched the controls. In order to jump from one realm of space to another, it was necessary to place the ship totally at rest in relation to its original domain. To fail to do so would build up kinetic energy which, when released by the jump, could result in a massive explosion.

'How are we doing?' Tedric asked Juvi.

'Fine,' she said. 'The computer says we're aligned. Any time you're ready, we are.'

'I'm ready,' said Tedric. 'I'm going to count down now. Twenty . . . nineteen . . . eighteen . . .'

Still, even as he counted the final seconds before the jump, Tedric's restless feeling persisted. He tried in vain to make sense of it. What might possibly be wrong? His eyes wandered through the cockpit, then stopped suddenly. Carey? he wondered. The man had said next to nothing since his release and now sat slack-jawed and blank faced. But who was he really? Watching Carey, Tedric's feeling grew stronger and stronger. Was this the same Matthew Carey whom Tedric had known so long or was it actually someone else, an imposter who . . .?

His own voice interrupted his thoughts. 'Three . . . two . . . one . . . zero.'

Juvi moved on signal, hitting the button. The ship jumped. The operation was instantaneous. In spite of the distortions of various tridee serials, there was no loud thundering boom; the ship didn't quake or bounce or shiver. Tedric looked at the viewscreen. The huge ball of a planet floated in front of his eyes.

'Tavera,' said Pal Galmain softly.

Tedric examined the planet. It was the same as the image

98

Skandos had shown him. Tavera proved to be an ugly, brown, pockmarked world. But Pal Galmain at least seemed genuinely moved by the sight. It was impossible not to sense the emotion he felt.

'Wilson,' said Tedric, turning in his seat, 'see if you can contact anyone. If you do, let Pal Galmain do the talking.'

'I will.' Wilson reached for the radio and, as he did, it finally happened. Tedric understood the exact meaning of his feeling. It was Carey, all right. Carey – and yet not Carey. It was Fra Villion. In a flash of enlightenment, Tedric understood who Fra Villion really was and what he presently intended. Tedric jumped from his seat with a yell and sprang across the room.

He was an instant too late. Carey's hand, moving with sudden speed, reached out and jerked the heatgun from the unsuspecting Ky-shan's holster. Thrusting past Wilson, Carey shoved the barrel against the radio console and fired one harsh bolt. A cloud of smoke erupted into the air and sparks flew crazily. An instant later, Tedric hit Carey and sent him crashing to the floor. The heatgun skidded across the room. Tedric swung his arm and cracked Carey firmly on the jaw. Carey's head snapped back and his eyes folded shut.

'By the Lords of the Universe,' cried Wilson, standing in front of the radio, 'what did he do that for?'

'I doubt that he had much say in the matter,' Tedric said, climbing wearily to his feet.

'But why destroy the radio of all things?'

'I doubt if that was all he intended. In another few seconds he could have swung the heatgun around, destroyed the controls, and killed half of us before anyone reached him.'

'He must have lost his mind.'

Tedric shook his head slowly. 'No, I'm afraid it was more than that.'

'Tedric is correct.' Pal Galmain's voice boomed loudly. 'The fault is as much mine as anyone's. Poor Carey has been monitored by Fra Villion. He has been a spy in our midst

99

since he first arrived. The man should have been killed in the beginning.'

Tedric wasn't about to argue the merits of killing Carey at this late moment. He was still reeling in shock from the suddenness of the flash of insight that had allowed him to prevent Carey from inflicting additional damage on the ship and crew.

'Company,' said Juvi softly. Unlike the rest of them, she had remained dutifully at her station. 'Eight . . . nine . . . ten ships. They're coming towards us.'

'There's Fra Villion now,' Pal Galmain said bitterly.

'And we've got no way of calling him off,' said Wilson, indicating the broken radio.

'And no forceshield to protect us,' Galmain added. 'And no gun turrets to fight back.' He laughed suddenly and rocked on his feet. 'Fra Villion has beaten us already. I was vain to believe it could ever be otherwise.'

But Tedric wasn't quite so eager to surrender hope. 'Man your stations,' he told his crew. 'When they kill us, we'll be dead, but until then I intend to keep fighting. Juvi, get ready to soft-talk a crazy computer. I intend reaching Tavera whether it's in one piece or twenty pieces or half a . . .'

A loud explosion drowned out the rest of his words. The little ship trembled like a twig in the wind. Tedric staggered across the floor and fell into the control chair. He gripped the wheel and took hold of the throttle. Swallowing one deep soothing breath of air after another, Tedric fought to clear his mind. For what now lay ahead, he needed to be absolutely calm.

On the screen in front of him, he could see the tiny yellow blips of the advancing *vemplar* ships. Even as he observed their approach, his hands were moving. He jerked the throttle and twisted the wheel; he eased up on the throttle and spun the wheel in the opposite direction. He attempted to let instinct alone guide his actions. There wasn't time for thinking and pondering, evaluating and considering. Besides, if he could determine the one logical course to pursue, then so could the enemy ships – and their computers.

Logic was a path that could be followed by others, while illogic was an endless maze. In order to survive, Tedric must enter the maze.

'Juvi,' he said, 'inform the computer that we're going to land on the surface of Tavera. Tell it, no matter what happens in the interim, that's the goal we intend to reach.'

'I'll try,' she said, with a flash of a smile.

'The rest of you, strap down. Ky-shan, take care of Carey. If he wakes up, knock him out again. This ride's apt to be a rough one but I'd rather be bumped around than burned up.'

By now, the nearest of the enemy ships was close enough to open fire. Tedric's hands danced as he evaded the initial heatray bolts. Tractor beams swept out and he darted between them. The other enemy ships closed in and he tried to cut a path through and around them. It was illogic again – the endless maze – but it was working. The ship bobbed and weaved like a boxer intent upon tiring an opponent. Heatrays and tractor beams continued to assault the ship. Tedric could feel those blasts that came close and sense those that did not. He was reminded of the feeling he had had about Carey. Like then, he seemed to be standing above and apart from his own body, observing the universe through a more distant and accurate lens.

As the ship darted through the enemy formation, Tedric's hands were never at rest. Instinct and impulse assumed full command of his actions. Twice the ship shook from near misses. Once, Tedric could actually see the bright yellow glow through the porthole above his head. He put the ship into a series of spiral manoeuvres, each successive circle different from the one before. Then, once he had the enemy safely in tow, he straightened the wheel and ran for Tavera.

The *vemplar* ships were at least as fast as his own and certainly as capable of dexterous manoeuvring. But his hands seemed to have a will of their own. He had entered the maze and the enemy was lost in his wake.

The cockpit remained hushed. Only Juvi occasionally broke the silence. 'Ship on our tail,' she said, and Tedric's hands moved in response. 'Two straight above with tractor beams,' and Tedric let the ship drop a hundred kilometres. 'Four intersecting at nine o'clock,' and Tedric's hands instinctively chose a six o'clock plunge.

On and on it went. Because he couldn't outrun them, Tedric had to take constant evasive action. One mistake, he knew, one wrong turn of the wheel or jerk of the throttle, and they would all be ash. Occasionally, lifting his head and opening his eyes, he glanced at the main viewscreen, and each time he did, the globe of Tavera loomed larger. They came closer . . . closer . . . closer . . .

Finally, Juvi said, 'We're in the atmosphere.'

Tedric looked at the screen in surprise and saw nothing but a broad expanse of brown. She was right: they had arrived.

'We'll burn up,' Pal Galmain warned softly. 'You'd better ease up on our speed.'

Tedric nodded, ordering his hands to duty. The ship was out of the maze, and now it was time to reassert conscious control. 'Juvi,' he said, 'have the computer scan the planetary surface. I want to locate this castle and bring us down as close to it as possible.'

'Fra Villion will tear his fur out by the roots when he sees us coming for dinner,' Juvi said happily as she moved to obey his command.

The others laughed at her joke. Even Pal Galmain cracked a smile. Tedric was gratified by their reaction. This victory, if that was indeed what it could be called, belonged equally to all of them. Their lives as well as his had been spared by mysterious forces he could not yet fully comprehend.

A mile or so above the surface of Tavera, Tedric levelled off the ship's plunging descent and turned parallel to the ground. The land beneath was a flat, dusty, heavily cratered plain, with only occasional pockets of scrub vegetation to indicate that life existed amid the desolation. Pal Galmain, watching on the screen, confirmed what Tedric had already guessed. 'Do not expect to find anything of interest out here. The planet is a vast wasteland. The only civilization on

Tavera is found within the walls of the castle Sanctuary. We *vemplars* prefer to make our own world, without the help of foolish nature.' Galmain's voice filled with pride as he spoke, and Tedric was reminded that no matter how amiable he sometimes seemed on the surface, underneath, where it mattered, Pal Galmian remained a dedicated and devout *vemplar*.

The enemy ships that had intercepted them in space continued their dogged pursuit. The computer, having discovered the location of the *vemplar* castle, was now urging the ship in that direction, but Tedric doubted they would ever reach their goal, a good quarter of the way around the globe. While the ships behind would not be likely to catch up, he expected that more would soon appear, and the limited range of the sky above this one planet would not provide sufficient manoeuvring room for him to duplicate the feat he had pulled off in space.

Wilson's thoughts seemed to be running in a similar line. He met Tedric's gaze and shook his head. 'Villion will undoubtedly send further ships against us, and it won't be so easy to get away from the next bunch. It's clear he wants us dead. Why should he quit now, when he's got us pinned down in his own back yard?'

'Couldn't we land?' Yod Cartwright suggested, looking at the screen.

Wilson shook his head. 'We'd be burned on the ground rather than the sky. It may make a difference to you, but as far as this old robot's concerned, one form of death is pretty much as permanent as another.'

'I didn't mean after they'd spotted us,' said Yod. 'I meant now. We could try to march overland to the castle.'

Tedric shook his head this time. 'I've considered that myself, but it's too far. Besides, it doesn't appear there's sufficient natural food on Tavera to sustain us for more than a few dozen miles. I don't think we could ever hope to walk a thousand.' Tedric let his eyes fall on Pal Galmain. The *vemplar* had a strained look on his face, as though he had been concentrating. 'Pal Galmain, this is your world. What do you think? Is there a way out for us?'

Galmain nodded slowly. 'There is one possibility. Since Villion has undoubtedly poisoned the minds of the other knights with lies, if they could be made aware of the truth, I think the attack would cease. As a *vemplar* – even an exiled one – I have a right under the ancient code to present my charges against Villion.'

'But how can that be done,' Tedric said, 'without a radio?' He kept glancing at the screen, expecting at any moment to discover the presence of additional ships.

'We *vemplars* possess certain mental powers. Among these, at the highest level of knighthood, is the ability to project one's image across broad expanses of space. It would be relatively simple for me to reach the castle and attempt to find help. However, I expect that Villion is in personal charge of this attack. Our ship would more than likely be destroyed – and my body with it – before I could succeed in convincing the others of his treachery.'

Tedric recalled that the first time he had seen Fra Villion it had been his image he had actually confronted. Yod Cartwright had proved that by firing a heatgun at Villion to no avail. 'Is there any other possibility?' asked Tedric.

'Only this,' Pal Galmain said. 'There are ships behind us and soon, I expect, ships ahead of us. All will possess means of communicating among themselves. If I could project my image into one of the ships and state my case, it might be possible to receive a favourable hearing, end this assault, and guarantee our safe passage to the castle.'

'Will you try it?' asked Tedric.

'The effort will be difficult. Their ships are in motion, as is ours. It will be a delicate, perhaps impossible task. Also, for me to make the attempt will necessitate leaving my body untended. Before I can consent to that, I will require your assurance to watch over me.'

'In what way?'

'There is a good chance this ship will be burned down or forced to crash before I can succeed in saving us. If that proves to be the case, I do not want my body to fall into the hands of Fra Villion.'

'May I ask why?'

'It is a question of pride. Villion, should he claim my corpse, would undoubtedly choose to display my head as a trophy. I want your promise to destroy my body in the event the need arises.'

'Then you have my word,' Tedric said, though he wasn't certain he would be able to fulfil his promise. If the ship did go down, he would more than likely be dead himself. Villion could then display as many heads as he wished.

Still, Galmain seemed satisfied. 'Then I will now attempt to save us all.'

'Will the other *vemplars* be able to recognise you? The way you look now isn't the way they'll remember you.'

Galmain smiled confidently. 'We knights have ways of identifying ourselves.'

'Then you ought . . .'

He broke off as Juvi spoke loudly. 'Ships ahead,' she said. 'I've spotted four already and there may be more.'

Tedric glanced down at the screen in front of him. He counted five ships approaching from ahead – then six. 'I'm going to dive,' he told them. 'We'll see if we can slip under them.' As he spoke, his eyes happened to pass Pal Galmain. The *vemplar*'s body stood as rigid as a statue. All the life had gone out of it.

But there was no time to think about Galmain. Either he would succeed in his effort or fail. Tedric could not help him now. The ship dived, but the enemy kept pace. In the viewscreen, the planetary surface rushed up at them like a big brown fist. Tedric came to a quick decision. 'We're going to have to land,' he announced. 'We may not stand any better chance down there than up here but it's the only hope we've got.'

Tedric brought the ship straight down, breaking the dive only at the last possible second. The ship struck belly-up and bounced across the soft ground, scattering a thick cloud of reddish dust.

'Let's make a dash for it,' Tedric said, leaping from his seat as soon as the ship came to a halt. 'Try to find cover – anything. Make them hunt for us.'

Juvi looked at the screen on her console. 'They're taking their time but they're coming. We won't get a hundred yards.'

Yod opened the lock and led the way out. Ky-shan followed, carrying the still unconscious form of Matthew Carey under one arm and the considerably heavier bulk of Pal Galmain under the other. Tedric was concerned about Carey's condition, but Ky-shan assured him that Carey had twice awakened during the flight through space. 'On both occasions, I laid him back to rest as you ordered, Lord Tedric.'

'If he wakes up again,' Tedric said, following the Wykzl through the lock, 'let him alone. Carey has as much right as any of us to witness his own death.'

The dust at their feet was soft and deep. Walking was extremely difficult and running next to impossible. As he trudged away from the ship, Tedric cocked an ear but the silence was total and ominous. The sky was a dingy shade of brownish grey, the air thin and filled with dust particles. Everywhere he could see, the land was flat and completely devoid of distinguishing features. Not a very pleasant place to live, he decided – or to die.

'I don't think we're going to find a place to hide,' Wilson said, from close behind Tedric. 'I think we ought to stop and make a stand.'

'They'll just burn us down from the air,' Yod Cartwright said.

Wilson shrugged. 'Probably. But do you have a better idea?'

'I guess I don't,' Yod admitted.

'Then we might as well die on our feet.'

Tedric knew Wilson was right. There was no reason to run with no place to hide. 'Let's form a defensive circle,' he said. 'Maybe, since they're knights, they'll give us a fighting chance.'

Wilson laughed bitterly but moved as directed. Tedric stood between Yod and Ky-shan, who still clutched the two unconscious bodies.

'I think I hear something,' Juvi said softly.

Tedric listened and heard it too. A shrill whistling sound, distant but growing louder in the vast silence. Several more minutes passed before the ships finally appeared. Two of them, moving slowly, hovering overhead, from which group he could not tell. Tedric removed his heatgun from its holster. The weapon was next to useless against armoured ships, but he felt comforted by its weight in his hand.

The two ships simply hung in the sky. At every passing moment, Tedric expected to see the glint of the yellow heatray lashing out to mark the end of his natural life. A third ship floated down and joined the others in a triangular formation.

'They're toying with us,' said Wilson. 'I'll bet they're all up there laughing.'

'I don't think Villion would want to take time for laughter,' Tedric said, feeling a dim flash of hope.

As if in response to his feeling, one of the ships fell away from the others. Tedric watched the smooth streamlined shape as it descended towards the ground.

'It's going to land,' Juvi said.

Tedric nodded. He glanced hopefully at Pal Galmain, but the *vemplar* was as rigid and lifeless in Ky-shan's grasp as before.

'Maybe it's Fra Villion himself come to gloat at our fate,' said Wilson, balancing his heatgun menacingly in his hand. 'If it is, I swear I'll kill the beast if it takes the strength of a hundred men.'

The ship came neatly to rest, dropping on its belly a few hundred yards from the watching circle. Three additional ships had joined those overhead. The formation moved in a stately circle.

'Someone's coming out,' said Yod.

Tedric saw a door in the side of the ship opening slowly. He raised his heatgun and took a slow breath. He knew it wouldn't likely be Villion. But who? A large, dark, sinister figure dressed in a black cape and jumpsuit emerged through the door. Automatically, Tedric felt his hand tighten on his gun.

'It is Fra Villion!' Yod cried, springing from the circle and rushing blindly forward, heatgun raised.

A booted foot lashed suddenly out of nowhere and sent the gun flying from his hand.

'It is not Fra Villion,' said Pal Galmain. 'That is Dol Watlat.'

The *vemplar* from the ship continued to advance at a steady pace.

'You made it!' cried Juvi, rushing forward and throwing her arms around Pal Galmain in a warm embrace. For a moment, Tedric actually thought he might have glimpsed a display of real emotion on the *vemplar*'s face, but it was over as soon as it had come.

Pal Galmain stepped back and bowed to Juvi. 'I was indeed able to complete my mission. I apologise for the delay, but it was a delicate operation, as I warned you it might be. Dol Watlat is an old *vemplar* who, fortunately, once knew me well. He will help us.'

The *vemplar* stopped in the dust a dozen paces away. The hilt of a whipsword showed in one hand. 'You, Pal Galmain, exiled traitor to your own blood oath, are hereby placed under official arrest and ordered to face judgment for the crime of willful disobedience to the terms of the ancient code.'

Wilson looked sceptically at Pal Galmain. 'This is the fellow who's going to help us?'

Galmain shrugged. 'I'm afraid it's the best treatment we can hope for, but at least we're alive. Dol Watlat will see that we reach Sanctuary. After that, it will be a question of who is to be believed, Fra Villion or myself.'

'Still, he's not going to be overjoyed to see us,' said Wilson.

'Maybe he really will tear out his fur by the roots,' said Juvi with a laugh.

'You must dispose of any weapons in your possession at once,' Dol Watlat said. 'Drop them where you stand and approach the ship with your arms in the air.'

Tedric let his heatgun slide from his hand. He would miss the weapon's comforting feel, but there appeared to be little choice in the matter.

Tedric trudged forward through the dust of Tavera.

CHAPTER 14

Judgment

The tableau was indeed an impressive one. In a basement cavern of the castle Sanctuary, the *vemplars* of Tavera had gathered to pass judgment on Pal Galmain, an exiled comrade recently returned with terrible accusations against another of their own, Fra Villion. Along the walls close to the high ceiling, bright torches burned brilliantly, casting wild shadowy patterns against the white stones of the floor.

Tedric was the only person present at the hearing who was not a *vemplar*. The knights – as many as three hundred strong – occupied tall chairs arranged in widening concentric circles. At the centre sat Pal Galmain, his hands folded in his lap, his back slumped, his human-like face utterly blank. Tedric stood at his side. He had been called to testify as a witness.

The questioning began with the first row of knights, where Fra Villion himself sat, although, when his turn came, he frowned and shook his head and did not choose to speak. Most of the others did, however, each standing and asking questions of Tedric until, seemingly satisfied, the knight resumed his seat and let the questioning pass to the next in line. As he answered their questions, which had quickly grown repetitive, Tedric let his gaze fall upon Fra Villion, who looked up and met his eyes. There was no real animosity in Villion's expression, nor in the faint smile that momentarily crossed his brightly coloured face. If anything, Villion seemed supremely confident. He and Tedric had met in battle once before, but no clear victor had emerged from that initial confrontation. Villion seemed to be saying that this time – on his own world, among his own kind – the outcome would be different.

Pal Galmain, on the other hand, looked like a sick and

beaten man. Part of the problem was undoubtedly simple exhaustion. Tedric assumed that the hearing had been convened hours earlier, immediately upon their arrival at the castle – and Galmain's human-sized form made him appear frail and weak among these huge hairy giants. Still, in the time he had been present in this room, Tedric had not heard Galmain offer a single word in his own defence. His demeanour was dreamy, as if he no longer understood or cared about the events swirling around him. Tedric was deeply concerned. Without Galmain's active assistance, he did not see how Villion could ever be brought down.

As for the others – Juvi, Ky-shan, Yod, Wilson and Matthew Carey – Tedric was uncertain of their exact whereabouts, though he assumed they were being held somewhere in the castle. He himself had at first been taken under guard to a small room far above this one and kept there until the summons had come for him to testify.

By now, the questioning had reached the farthest and final row of the knights. One *vemplar*, an exact replica of Fra Villion except for his pale face, was asking a series of questions. Tedric tried to concentrate on the knight's words. 'Would it be accurate to say that you personally are not in possession of any direct evidence linking Fra Villion with the darker forces of our universe?'

Tedric tried not to seem irritated. He had heard this same question several times before and answered it to the best of his ability. 'I can only repeat what I've already told you. Skandos, the Scientist, informed me directly that Fra Villion was in the employ of these forces. I also believe that Villion's activities in the Empire of Man constitute additional proof of where his current loyalties lie.'

'But where is this Skandos now?' the knight went on. 'If he is in possession of definite proof, why do you insist he will refuse to come forward and offer it?'

Tedric had answered that question, too. The manner in which the subject kept coming up convinced him that Villion had more than likely planted the question in a deliberate attempt to cast doubt upon the entire case against him. It was plain from what Tedric had seen and heard in this room that Villion's position among the *vemplars* was indeed a strong one, which might in part explain Pal Galmain's apparent despair. The old knight had been away from home a long time and might not have realised the enormity of the challenge he faced.

Once more, Tedric could only repeat what he had told the assembly before. 'Skandos is a Scientist and as such it is his sworn duty to avoid interfering in the affairs of the Galaxy whenever possible. He is an observer and teacher, not an active participant. That has always been the way of the Scientists. Everyone in this room must be aware of that.'

The knight smirked, as though he had scored a victory. 'Then you admit that we have only your word, that of a mere human, to support any of these charges against Fra Villion?'

'My word,' said Tedric, 'and that of Pal Galmain.'

The knight's smirk grew broader. It was clear that he regarded Pal Galmain's word as less than reliable and wanted to be sure this opinion was communicated to his fellow knights.

'There's also the matter of the red clouds,' Tedric went on stubbornly, deciding this was as good a time as any to reiterate the entire case. 'Fra Villion was seen to enter one cloud upon his departure from the Empire of Man. Later, he reappeared here among you. No one disputes that the clouds are tools of the darker forces. And I can offer you proof – sworn testimony – to confirm what I've said. If you'd care to wait several months, I can have witnesses brought here. It's even possible that Matthew Carey, once he has recovered from his recent ordeal, will be able to convince you that Villion did indeed enter the cloud.'

The knight shrugged. 'I can speak only for myself, but I fail to see the necessity for such testimony. Fra Villion has explained to us that he entered the cloud in an attempt to discover its true nature. Such a cloud presently threatens our realm. Fra Villion merely wished to aid his own species.'

'At a time when the entire Imperial fleet was attempting

to destroy him?' Tedric laughed and shook his head. 'If Fra Villion told you that, then he's a liar, and if you believe him, then you're fools.'

The knight's dark eyes flashed with anger. He started to voice a strong retort when Villion lifted a hand and wagged it languidly in the air. The knight fell immediately silent, leaving no question of where his loyalty lay. He sat down and the questioning passed to the next, only somewhat less overtly hostile interrogator.

As the questioning moved onward to its end, Tedric struggled against his own welling despair. It was clear that a majority of the knights supported Villion, and no amount of testimony was about to sway them otherwise. There were a significant few who, as Tedric continued to repeat his case, cast anxious, worried glances in Villion's direction, but not nearly enough to carry the day.

The last interrogator completed his questioning and sat down. There was a long moment of silence and Tedric did not know whether he was expected to go or stay. Then Dol Watlat started to come to his feet. Tedric recognised him in the nearest circle, seated directly across from Fra Villion.

Dol Watlat spoke to Pal Galmain. 'Have you anything to add in your defence, noble knight?'

Galmain raised his head as if only just now aware that he was being addressed. He shook his head weakly. 'I . . . no. Not as a defence. Tedric has spoken well on my behalf. The case against Fra Villion has been made as best it can.'

Tedric heard snickers around the hall.

'Then do you wish me to call a vote?' Dol Watlat said, his voice almost sad.

'Yes . . . no.' Galmain waved a hand. 'I can see that I am beaten. I have no desire to see Fra Villion given another triumph at my expense.'

'Then I must ask you to leave the room. The matter of your own crime in returning here must now be discussed.'

'No,' said Galmain, and suddenly his voice was loud. He rose to his feet slowly but once there stood proud and rigid. 'I have something I wish to say.'

'But you have already informed us that your case has rested,' said Dol Watlat in surprise.

Galmain shook his head. 'You misunderstand. I do not wish to address myself to the subject of my own defence. Rather, I wish to speak concerning you – all of you – and . . .' he paused and, turning sharply, pointed a finger at Villion '. . . and him.'

'This, as you know, Pal Galmain, is not an accepted part of the ritual of judgment.'

'True, but in this instance, I request a special dispensation. The fact is that I have come a long way to be among you. I am an old man and not well. Even if you sentence me to die, as I assume you will, I doubt that I will live long enough to give those of you who are my enemies the satisfaction of seeing my head severed from my body.'

'Then speak,' said Dol Watlat, sitting down. 'I at least will not refuse to hear you.'

Tedric glanced at Villion who, for a moment, seemed ready to raise a protest. Then he relaxed. It was clear that Villion no longer regarded Pal Galmain as a possible menace.

'Years ago, as most of you will recall,' Galmain began, 'I was an acknowledged leader among the black knights of Tavera, the Biomen *vemplar*.' His voice showed no indication of hesitancy now. He appeared to have discovered a hidden reserve of strength and was putting it into his words. 'I was proud of my position and proud of my colleagues. The blood oath of the ancient code served us and served us well. There were many who hated us. Even among our own kind, the Biomen, we were often regarded with fear and distrust. It was said that we were amoral, lacking in principle, but I believed, as all of you did, that the ancient code constituted a higher principle of loyalty, devotion, and trust that loomed far above the mere temporal affairs of the Galaxy.' Turning his head, he stared fixedly at Villion. 'I now admit that I was wrong. There is one among you who has brought shame to your ranks and confirmed the judgments made by others. This individual has proved at long last that the ancient code is a limited creed. In my opinion, the salvation of the universe we all inhabit must take precedence over any blood oath. Fra Villion appears to dispute this claim.'

Tedric heard a sharp intake of breath but he could not immediately identify its source.

'In his heart,' Galmain went on, his expression intent, 'Fra Villion undoubtedly believes that he is correct in continuing to obey the code. When he first accepted employment from the darker forces, Fra Villion . . .'

Galmain was forced to break off as a general murmur of discontent sounded through the room. He waited until it had ebbed, then said, 'I am fully aware of how most of you pretend to believe but at the moment I do not care. To me, the facts are plain to all who are not blind and I prefer not to argue them now. I know that I was approached with an offer of employment, which I refused. Fra Villion was later approached similarly and he, for whatever reasons, accepted. He has since served his masters to the best of his ability. If the universe falls as a result, he will no doubt continue to believe that the ancient code required him to act as he did.'

Galmain, pausing, took a deep breath and appeared to waver on his feet. It was clear that the old knight was seriously ill and that it was not simply a matter of exhaustion. For his part, Villion seemed unmoved by Galmain's bitter words. His features were as cool as ever, though the smile had vanished from his lips, at least for the time being.

'Because of this,' Galmain went on, his strength asserting itself again, 'it is clear that in his own opinion Fra Villion has committed no crime. You, in your actions today, have apparently confirmed this judgment. Therefore, only one thing can possibly save the universe and release Fra Villion from a position he may very well no longer wish to hold. To that end, out of my respect for him and my devotion to you, I offer Fra Villion the challenge of a duel to the death.'

These last words seemed to catch the entire assembly by surprise. There was a loud gasp of amazement and then, from a few, openly derisive laughter. Pal Galmain stood his ground with dignity.

'Fra Villion,' he said, 'I have offered myself to you in a duel to the death. What is your response?'

Villion looked distinctly uncomfortable. He shook his head and, for the first time since Tedric had been present, spoke directly to Galmain. 'No, old knight, you are too ill. A duel to the death between us could have only one conceivable outcome. I am no executioner. You must wait for the axe.'

Pal Galmain frowned as if deeply offended. 'That decision is not yours to make, Fra Villion. I repeat my challenge. According to the terms of the ancient code, you must either accept or refuse. If you refuse, you are branded a coward and no longer fit to serve among the black knights.'

'You intend to press this ridiculous challenge?' said Villion.

'The choice of weapons is yours to make.'

Villion shifted his gaze. It was clear that he was seeking some avenue of escape but none was presented to him. He sighed. 'The traditional weapons, then. Whipswords. But I am indeed sorry. Once you were a great and noble *vemplar*, Pal Galmain. Now . . .'

'We will meet at dawn, Fra Villion.'

With that, moving stiffly, Pal Galmain stepped away. The assembled knights shifted aside to allow him to pass. Tedric went after him. He knew that Villion was undoubtedly correct – Galmain would never survive a duel to the death, not in his present condition – but he deeply admired the old knight for his valiant if futile gesture.

Pal Galmain reached the door at the rear of the cavern and passed through it. Tedric followed. Outside, at the foot of a stone staircase, two knights were already waiting to escort them. Pal Galmain brushed swiftly past them. The *vemplars* waited a moment and then followed at a discreet distance.

Halfway up the stairs, Pal Galmain suddenly faltered and the whole of his weight fell against Tedric. The *vemplar*'s face was pale and his skin covered in sweat. 'You'll have to help me,' he said in a weak voice. 'Take me to your room. Can you find it? Don't let them see me like this.'

'I can find it,' said Tedric. He let Pal Galmain hold his arm as they continued to ascend the stairs. It seemed a long, long way to the top.

CHAPTER 15

The Adversary

By the time the two of them reached the room Tedric had been assigned in the upper reaches of the castle Sanctuary, Pal Galmain seemed on the verge of total collapse. Tedric assisted the old knight through the door and guided him to the bed, where Galmain lay down with a heavy groan. Turning, Tedric started to go in search of help when Pal Galmain, suddenly alert again, called him back.

'I want to make them help you,' Tedric said.

'No – don't. Close the door and stay here.' Galmain's face was even paler than before, and deeply engrained lines and wrinkles showed in his neck and brow. For the first time since Tedric had known him, Galmain actually looked like what he was: an old, sick man.

'You need medical attention,' Tedric said. 'They must have a physician here somewhere.' But he shut the door and then came back to the bed.

Galmain nodded and relaxed. His eyes fell shut; his breathing was soft. 'You don't understand. There's no point . . . no need.' Struggling suddenly, he clasped Tedric's sleeve and tugged at the fabric. 'If they – Villion – if he knows I'm ill, it'll provide him the excuse he wants to avoid the duel.'

'You can't hope to fight him in your present condition. It would be suicide.'

'No. I'll be better. A little rest. That's all I need. A few hours sleep.'

Tedric shook his head. He didn't want to tell Galmain the truth, that he didn't stand a chance against Villion. Tedric had once engaged Villion with whipswords and he knew the depth of the *vemplar*'s skill. Tedric had emerged from that fight with at least a stand-off, but he was young and strong and Pal Galmain was neither. 'We can delay the duel,' he suggested, 'until you're recovered. It doesn't have to be fought tomorrow.'

'No!' Galmain's voice was desperate. 'You don't understand. Yes, I'm sick. Yes, I'm going to die. That's the reason it's necessary to hurry. I know a way – a weakness. I can beat Villion. He was once my pupil, you remember. I taught him the art of combat. When he was only a child, a boy, we danced for hours in the courtyard below, and even when night fell and neither of us could see the other, we continued. I taught Fra Villion everything I knew until he had surpassed me in every respect but one. That one thing will allow me to destroy him.'

'I see,' said Tedric, who did not know whether to believe the old knight's assertion. Galmain was undoubtedly ill. His mind might not be right. Perhaps he was dreaming things that no longer existed and perhaps never had.

Galmain, sensing Tedric's hesitation, struggled to smile. 'Here, lean close,' he said, 'and I'll tell you what I mean. Once you know, you'll have to believe me.'

Tedric bent close to the bed, feeling Galmain's breath against his ear. The old knight whispered gently. Tedric listened intently. When Galmain finished, he stood upright and pondered for a long moment. A voice from behind interrupted his thoughts.

'What have they done to him?'

Tedric turned. Juvi, Yod, and Wilson stood just inside the door. It was Juvi who had spoken.

'He's sick,' she said.

Tedric related what had occurred in the basement cavern. 'Pal Galmain has challenged Villion to a whipsword duel to be fought tomorrow at dawn,' he finished.

Juvi looked shocked. 'That's pure madness. Can't they see how sick he is? I'm going to get help for him.'

'No,' Galmain said, but his voice was much weaker now. He opened an eye and looked imploringly at Tedric. 'Tell her she shouldn't.'

But Juvi was determined and Tedric did not try to stop

her. She swept out of the room and he could hear her angry voice in the hallway as she apparently argued with some of the *vemplar* guards. Galmain had again fallen back on the bed. His face was slack. Tedric turned to Yod and Wilson. 'Well, what's been happening with you?'

'We've got rooms further down the corridor,' Wilson said. He looked worriedly at Galmain as he spoke. The *vemplar* was apparently asleep now. 'They don't mind if we roam around up here, but try and go below and they stop you.'

'What about Ky-shan?'

'He's got a room, too. Juvi heard your voice, so we came down here. What you said about that trial was pretty bad news. It looks as though we've wasted our time and effort coming here.'

'I don't think it's totally hopeless yet,' said Tedric, though he feared he was only being stubbornly optimistic. 'What about Matthew Carey? Has his condition improved?'

Wilson shrugged. 'That's hard to say. He's awake and talking, but . . .' He tapped the side of his head meaningfully. 'I think whatever Villion did – taking over his mind – it's left poor Carey scrambled. He doesn't seem to have any idea what's going on.'

'He's not faking?'

Wilson shook his head. 'No. It's real, I'm afraid.'

Tedric knew what that meant. Yet another possibility had vanished. He had hoped to convince Carey to speak the truth to the assembled knights. He, more than anyone, knew the factual details concerning Villion's relationship with the darker forces, but now, if Wilson was correct, even that slim hope had been erased.

Tedric let his gaze return to the bed. Galmain was definitely unconscious, his breathing shallow. All at once, Tedric was certain that the old knight would never awaken. It had taken all the will he possessed to come this far, and when that great effort had proved in vain – when his former comrades had treated him as a liar – he had lost the strength to continue fighting. The challenge to Villion was a final desperate attempt to assert his will, but it had been too little, too late.

The sound of stumbling footsteps made Tedric turn. Matthew Carey stood in the doorway. As soon as Tedric saw him, he knew that Wilson had spoken the truth. Carey's eyes were as round and white as saucers. His lips moved but no sound emerged. The muscles in one cheek twitched crazily.

Tedric went over and placed a hand on Carey's shoulder. 'Come, Matthew, there's nothing for you here.'

'Who . . . who's that?' Carey pointed at the bed.

'Just a friend.'

His head jerked on his shoulders. 'Who are you?'

'Tedric.'

'Tedric?' Carey said the word musingly, as if trying to determine its meaning from the sound alone. He shrugged. 'No, I'm afraid I don't know any Tedric.'

'Come along, Matthew. You need to rest.'

Tedric led Carey gently through the door. Carey seemed quite willing to go wherever Tedric chose to take him. In the corridor, Tedric looked around for any sign of Juvi, but she had apparently gone below. Two *vemplars* stood at the head of the staircase, but Tedric didn't bother trying to approach them now. 'Which room is yours?' he asked Carey.

'Room?' He shook his head rapidly. 'I have no room. They won't . . . they can't . . .'

His voice faded into an indecipherable murmur. Tedric led him to the first open door and took him through. Ky-shan was there, standing alone in the middle of the room.

'Ky-shan, can you watch Matthew? He doesn't seem well.'

Carey was staring at the giant blue alien as though he'd never seen such a sight in his life. 'What a horrible looking monster!' he exclaimed.

'Ky-shan is a friend, too,' Tedric reassured him.

'If you say so.' Carey seemed less than convinced. He approached the bed cautiously, tiptoeing past Ky-shan, then dropped down suddenly on the soft mattress. His movements were jerky and exaggerated, like a puppet on strings. He threw back his head, kicked both legs, and lay prone. In a moment, he seemed fast asleep.

'That man is deeply disturbed mentally, Lord Tedric,' Ky-shan said.

'I know. It's Villion's doing, like so much else. I don't believe Carey's dangerous, though. Keep him here and watch over him. If you need help, the rest of us are in a room farther up the corridor. Pal Galmain is ill. I'm afraid he may be dying.'

'Then it went poorly with the knights, Lord Tedric?'

'It did indeed, Ky-shan. The *vemplars* refused to believe anything we told them. It appears that Fra Villion's position here is unassailable.'

'Then we will have to fight our way out?'

'I don't know about that either. Frankly, if we fail here, there may be nothing left to fight our way back to.'

Tedric went into the corridor. He heard Juvi's voice from the room ahead and assumed she'd returned with medical help for Galmain. It was clear now that the duel to the death between the two *vemplars* would never take place. That was a disappointment too, Tedric thought. What Galmain had revealed to him about Villion's supposed weakness had had a definite ring of truth to it.

Tedric was about to step into the room when a sharp hissing sound caught his attention. Glancing across the corridor, he discovered a beautiful blonde woman dressed like a *vemplar* huddled in the opposite doorway. It took him a moment to recognise Lola Dass, whom he had seen only briefly in the past.

'Tedric,' she said, in a soft whisper, 'come closer. I have things to tell you.'

Tedric glanced down the corridor. The two *vemplars* he had noticed before were no longer in sight, though he did not doubt that they remained nearby. He darted across the corridor and stood close beside the woman. 'What do you want with me?'

'It's not what I want of you, Tedric. It's what you need from me. I can help you and no one else can.'

Tedric was fully aware of Lola's intimate involvement with Fra Villion and had no reason to believe that the nature of their relationship had altered. If she was here on Tavera, that was a firm indication that it had not.

'You're Villion's friend,' he said. 'I don't think it's likely you can help me now.'

She smiled at the stiffness of his tone and touched his arm gently. 'You're too harsh with me, Tedric. I despise Villion as much as you or anyone. I've lived on this planet for months. I know how horrible it can be. I want to get out of here. So do you. That gives us something in common.'

'I'm not sure if it does or not. Our reasons for wishing to leave Tavera are too different.'

'Villion deceived me, tricked me. Do you think I came here of my own free will? You saw what he did to Carey. Well, it was the same with me. Villion took control of my mind and forced me to do his bidding.'

Tedric didn't believe a word she was saying. He had seen Lola at Villion's side aboard the Iron Sphere. No one had controlled her mind then. Still, he saw no reason to reject her advances outright. 'What exactly is it that you propose to do?'

'There's only one thing that matters – getting off this planet and getting home to Earth where we belong.'

Tedric shook his head. 'Right now, the Earth is no good place to be either.'

'If you're talking about the red cloud that drives people insane, I know about it.' She bit her lip and for the first time looked genuinely anxious.

'How do you know about it?' he asked.

'In ways that neither you nor Villion could guess,' she said smugly. Leaning past Tedric, she glanced up the corridor. It was deserted and she seemed to make a decision. 'Come with me and I'll show you what I mean.'

He hesitated, not trusting her. 'Come where?'

'To Fra Villion's secret hideaway. He has a friend there with him. When we arrive, you'll see what I mean.'

Tedric allowed Lola to lead him down the corridor. She kept close to the wall and glanced frequently behind, but the hallway remained vacant until they reached its end, a solid stone wall. Lola paused and reached out quickly. With the knuckles of one hand, she rapped hard twice against one section. The wall gave a sudden, loud groan and swung slowly back on a set of invisible hinges. Lola laughed softly in delight and slipped into the darkness beyond. Tedric, after a moment's hesitation, followed. As soon as he had, the wall automatically swung shut behind him. They were surrounded by thick, impenetrable blackness.

Her fingers closed around his hand. 'Stay close to me. I know the way. Villion brought me here first, but I've done some exploring on my own since.'

The floor slanted downward. Tedric moved with caution, letting Lola guide him. She seemed to possess eyes that could see in the dark, like certain breeds of subwoman. The passageway moved downward in a series of descending circles. Tedric received the impression that there were other passageways branching off from this one.

'It's an entire secret system,' she said, confirming his judgment. 'It goes all the way through the castle. If you want, you can go almost anywhere. I watched that trial in the basement. It was laughable. No matter how much Villion lies, those fools believe him.'

'Does anyone know about this besides you and Villion?'

'I doubt it. Villion's no fool. He loves to spy on others, but he wouldn't care for it if they spied on him.'

'But you are.'

She laughed. 'He trusted me once.'

Tedric intended to make it a point not to repeat Villion's error. He had no idea how far they'd come when Lola moved onto one of the side passageways. The floor no longer slanted. 'It's right down here,' she said, whispering now. 'We'll have to be very quiet. I hope Villion's still there. When I left to get you, he was still waiting for his friend.'

A short distance farther on, she halted and he heard her fingers moving against the wall. Suddenly, there was a burst of gentle light and he could see again. There was a dimly lit room in front of him. Except for a solitary figure standing in the middle of the floor, the room was empty.

That figure was Fra Villion.

Tedric jumped back in surprise, but Lola gripped his arm and squeezed reassuringly. Then he understood. The wall had not vanished. What he was seeing was only a picture on a screen. They were watching Villion but he could not see them.

Lola's hand fumbled at the wall again. A voice rose around them. It was Fra Villion. His words grew slowly in volume. Tedric peered at the screen more closely. Villion was talking, yes, but to whom? As far as Tedric could tell, the knight was unquestionably alone in the room.

Tedric listened to what Villion was saying. His voice was querulous, as though engaged in an argument. 'I tell you there's nothing more to fear. Old Galmain is dying. I sent my own physician to see him and he assured me there's absolutely no hope. If Galmain dies now, it couldn't be better. That ridiculous duel might have wounded my position in the eyes of the others.'

Tedric still didn't know who or what Villion was addressing. He turned to ask Lola, but her fearful touch convinced him to remain silent. If Villion discovered them here, it would be she who would suffer the most.

A voice answered Villion. It did not speak aloud. Tedric heard the voice only in his mind, not in his ears. It said: *The fate of Pal Galmain is of no concern to us. He is your enemy, not ours. We want Tedric destroyed and only Tedric. If you kill others, that is your private affair.*

Villion still sounded angry. 'I've already explained how I intend to deal with Tedric. He and the others with him are simple intruders. They will be dealt with as such and executed.'

Tedric wasn't especially surprised to hear this. He had long since expected something of the sort. It was the other voice, the silent one, that continued to disturb him. Who could it be? As far as he knew, only the Scientists possessed the ability to communicate through their minds alone, and he was certain this creature was not one of them.

Laughter sounded in his head. *Villion, don't you learn? Again, you are underestimating our friend Tedric. His death will not come as easily as you think. He is a strong and powerful force. Only a fool would fail to regard him as such.*

Tedric now realised whose voice this was. The realisation came as no great surprise, as if he had been anticipating this confrontation all along. What he was hearing was the disembodied voice of a member of the darker forces – of an adversary.

Tedric felt his lips twist into a smile. In the years he had spent in this universe in conflict with these mysterious creatures, he had never been so close to one before. From the familiar way in which it spoke, the adversary plainly knew Tedric well. Now was his chance to even the score.

'Tedric is no more powerful than any human being,' Villion said. 'He's physically strong, a fine warrior, I grant you that, but only a barbarian, a savage even among the denizens of the Empire. To come here to Tavera as Tedric did can only be regarded as an act of foolishness.'

Or courage, said the voice. *Perhaps you ought to consider that possibility, Fra Villion.*

'I have considered it. The difference between bravery and stupidity is minute. No matter. Tedric will not leave Tavera alive.'

The voice laughed. *Or, as you say, it will be over your dead body? Is that correct, Fra Villion? Well, we shall see. Indeed, we shall see.*

The creature had gone. Tedric was somehow certain of that. He observed Fra Villion. For a considerable time, the *vemplar* stood without moving in the middle of the room. Whether he was considering the voice's parting words, Tedric could not tell. Then Villion vanished. Tedric had witnessed this trick before and felt no surprise.

'Well, what do you think?' said Lola, after a moment.

Tedric answered evasively, uncertain how much she knew about the true nature of the adversary. 'I'm not sure what to think.'

She sounded irritated. 'Isn't it obvious? Villion's gone crazy. He's out of his mind. You saw him the same as I did. He stands in the middle of a room, talking to himself. Something's wrong with him. That's for sure.'

'What do you mean?' Tedric said. 'Didn't you hear the voice?'

'I heard Villion but . . .'

'And not the other? You didn't hear a voice inside your head?'

He could feel her looking at him with suspicion even if he couldn't actually see her expression. 'You're playing with me, aren't you? What's the joke?'

'You heard nothing?'

'Not a damn thing. Only Villion.'

Tedric forced a laugh. There was no disputing her sincerity. 'I'm sorry. I was joking. I shouldn't have done that.'

She still sounded suspicious. 'I brought you here so that you could see that Villion was cracking up, not to have fun at my expense. I thought you'd appreciate my help. If I was mistaken. . .'

'No, don't think that.' He caught her arm in his grip. 'I'm grateful for what you did. It may turn out to be extremely important. If you could tell the knights exactly what you saw here, then we might . . .'

'Oh, no you don't,' she said, jerking away from him. 'I'm not the one who's crazy. I'm not telling anybody anything.'

'It could possibly save all our lives.'

'The life I'm most concerned with is my own. If I go telling tales on Fra Villion, he'll put my neck under the executioner's axe.'

'I thought you wanted to help.'

'That doesn't mean I intend to be stupid about it.'

He sighed, recognising the futility of trying to argue

further with her. 'All right. If that's the way you want it, we'd better get back.'

'I'm sorry, but that's the way it's got to be,' she confirmed.

Again, he let her guide him through the darkness. Soon, the floor slanted upwards beneath his feet and they ascended.

Eventually, stopping, she said, 'All right, this is where we started out.'

'I'd better get back to the others.'

'You won't forget your promise to me? You said, if I helped you, you'd get me out of here.'

Tedric didn't recall making any such promise. 'I'll do what I can, Lola. With your help . . .'

'No,' she said firmly. 'I won't talk to anyone.'

'Then I can only promise that I won't leave Tavera without you.'

'I guess that'll have to be enough.' She edged closer to him until he could feel her warm body pressing against him. 'I'll be in contact,' she said.

Sliding away, she touched the wall, activating another of the screens. Through it, Tedric could see the corridor, which was empty. Reaching out, Lola tapped the wall twice. It swung open on its hinges and Tedric stepped through. Turning, he watched her wave in farewell. Standing there, she resembled nothing more than a frail, frightened young girl. He wondered how someone so lovely on the outside could at the same time be so ugly within.

As he moved down the corridor, Tedric saw Juvi emerge from his room and hurry towards him. Her head was down and she didn't appear to see him. Reaching out, he caught her arm. She looked up at him and her eyes were filled with tears.

'He's dead,' she said. 'There wasn't a thing we could do to help. He just lay there sleeping and never woke up.'

He released her and hurried into the room. A Bioman, the physician apparently, crouched beside the bed. As soon as Tedric looked at the face of the man on the bed, he knew Juvi had told the truth.

Pal Galmain was indeed dead.

CHAPTER 16

Duel to the Death

After Pal Galmain's body had been removed by a *vemplar* guard, Tedric asked the others to return to their rooms so that he could have time to be alone and think. As the day passed from evening into night – the period of rotation for Tavera appeared to be approximately twenty Earth hours – Tedric remained by himself. A female servant, the first Biowoman Tedric had ever seen, appeared with a tray of food, but he sent her away to tend to the others. Juvi visited him once, but he was in no mood to talk, and she soon left. Somewhat later, Wilson came by but stayed only a short time and did not disturb Tedric's concentration with what were, as yet, still unanswerable questions.

As the hours passed, one thing stood out clearly in his mind and that was the fact that Lola Dass had not heard the voice of the adversary. To Tedric, this could have only two possible interpretations. Either he, himself, was possessed of some previously unrecognised special talent that permitted him to hear mental voices or else the adversary had known of his presence and deliberately directed its voice so that Tedric, as well as Villion, could hear. If the latter supposition was correct, it raised a number of interesting possibilities. For one thing, if the adversary was aware of Tedric's presence, why had it failed to warn Villion?

Tedric pondered these questions and others as the night progressed and arrived at a number of tentative conclusions. He thought it very likely that the adversaries resembled their enemies, the Scientists, in more ways than Skandos realised and were perhaps not so eager to interfere in Galactic affairs as was sometimes suspected. While the adversaries might favour their agent, Villion, in any confrontation with Tedric – as Skandos would surely favour Tedric – it was very possible that they would not elect to interfere directly to affect the eventual outcome. For Tedric, if true, this was the most promising thing he had discovered since his arrival on Tavera.

As the first faint rays of dawn came slicing through the window of his room, Tedric heard heavy footsteps in the corridor, and a moment later the door thrust open and a delegation of a dozen or so *vemplars* were standing at attention on his doorstep. The knight at the head of the group spoke stiffly: 'We have come to escort the former knight, Pal Galmain, to the assembly of *vemplars*.'

Tedric was surprised that the knight was unaware of Galmain's death, then realised the truth. He did know. This was merely part of some ritual that had to be played to its final end. Tedric decided to take advantage of this fact.

'Pal Galmain is no longer available,' he said. 'He is dead.'

The *vemplar* showed no particular surprise, a reaction that confirmed Tedric's judgment. 'In that event . . .'

'But, before he died, he asked me to take his place today.' Tedric came to his feet as he spoke.

The *vemplar* looked confused. 'We were instructed to escort Pal Galmain and only Pal Galmain.'

'And Galmain is dead. Surely, you would not choose to violate his last wishes.'

The knight seemed unable to decide. He looked at the others but their blank faces offered no assistance.

Tedric decided to help: 'Why don't you take me below and let the assembly decide whether I can stay?'

The *vemplar* appeared willing to accept this compromise. He motioned to the others, and Tedric joined them in the hall. The delegation had reached the head of the stairs when Tedric suddenly paused.

'I nearly forgot,' he told the *vemplar*. 'Pal Galmain also wished that the others in my group be present today. Would you mind sending someone back for them?'

Tedric had anticipated considerable resistance, which was the reason he had delayed making the request, but the knight seemed so thoroughly confused by now that he sent one of his men away immediately.

A short time later, Yod, Juvi, Wilson Ky-shan, and Matthew Carey emerged from their various rooms. Yod and Juvi looked sleepy, Wilson was curious, Ky-shan stoic, and Carey as blank and bemused as ever. The group moved down the stairs.

In the basement cavern below, the *vemplars* of Tavera had assembled once more. When the procession entered the room, the knights in the rear turned and stared curiously. Tedric wondered what Villion's reaction would be, but he was too far away to be seen.

'Stay here,' Tedric told the knight who had brought him. 'I'll go ahead by myself.'

Without waiting for a reply, he moved into the circle of knights. Chairs slid hastily aside to allow him to pass. When he reached the vacant centre of the assembly, he turned and looked at Fra Villion for the first time. Villion's rainbow face reflected surprise, puzzlement, anger, hatred, and – Tedric thought – perhaps a small quotient of fear.

Under Tedric's gaze, Villion sprang to his feet. 'What is the meaning of this?' he cried, addressing the entire assembly. 'A delegation was sent to bring Pal Galmain to face his former comrades. What is this human doing here?'

'Galmain is dead,' Tedric said.

Villion spun on him. 'We know that. It fails to explain your presence.'

'I'll be glad to do that.' Tedric gazed past the heads of the seated *vemplars* and saw the members of his crew standing against the wall nearest the door. 'Before his death, Pal Galmain spoke to me in confidence and requested that I fulfil his outstanding obligations. I made that promise to a man who had been my friend and I do intend to keep it. As a result, I have come here this morning to keep an appointment. You and I, Fra Villion, are scheduled to engage in a duel to the death.'

Villion looked furious. He struggled to emit a laugh. 'That

is absolutely absurd,' he said smugly. 'Pal Galmain was once a *vemplar*. He can issue such a challenge. You cannot.'

'I am not challenging you. Galmain already has. As I explained, I am here only to fulfil his commitment. It's as simple as that, Fra Villion.'

'And as ridiculous.'

Tedric decided it was his turn to address the gathering. He spoke forcefully. 'What is the problem with you, Fra Villion? Do I detect a certain hesitancy from you? You and I have locked whipswords in the past. Is it possible you are afraid to grant me a re-match?'

The suggestion of cowardice on Villion's part seemed to send a wave of shock rebounding through the room. Villion again tried to laugh, but there was nothing amused in his expression. 'When we met before, Tedric, you were afforded certain advantages. This time, since it is a duel to the death among *vemplars*, I could grant you nothing.'

'If you're talking about your ability to leap through space, I am aware of that and have no particular fear. Fight your battle as you wish and I shall fight mine in the same way.' He let his eyes roam the room quickly. 'If these chairs could be cleared aside, we might begin now.'

Villion looked frantic. 'You are a fool. You are begging to be killed.'

'Since my neck is already intended for the executioner's axe, it would appear that I have little to lose.'

As he spoke, Tedric observed Villion's face carefully. The reference to the executioner's axe sent a flutter of concern across his face. Plainly, Villion was wondering exactly how Tedric had come to know that.

'Either fight me now, Fra Villion,' said Tedric, 'or else surrender your chair among the knights. By the blood oath of your ancient code, you have no other choice.'

Villion's eyes went cold. 'Then we shall fight, Tedric, and you shall die.' He removed the whipsword from around his waist and waved the handle in the air. 'Move these chairs,' he commanded. 'The duel will be fought here and fought now.'

Tedric waited patiently while the knights cleared the floor. The *vemplar* who had brought him here approached diffidently and offered Tedric the use of his sword. The weapon, which Tedric had used only once before – against Villion – possessed a long, extremely thin blade, like a piece of taut wire, that was capable of sheering off a man's head with a single flick of the wrist. Tedric pressed a button in the wooden handle of the sword and let the blade wave freely. He shook his wrist and listened as the sword whistled shrilly through the air.

Tedric nodded in satisfaction, closed the sword, and thanked the knight for the gift. He then went over to where the others in his group were standing and said, 'I don't want you to attempt to interfere in this. No matter what happens, stay where you are and hope for the best.' He grinned in a sudden show of confidence. 'Once Villion is dead, we can all go home.'

Yod Cartwright looked awed, Juvi worried, Wilson admiring, Ky-shan stoic, and Matthew Carey insensible. Tedric placed a hand on Carey's shoulder. 'Stay close to the others, Matthew. No matter what happens to me, they'll take care of you. They're your friends. Do you understand?'

As wide-eyed as a child, Carey looked up and nodded. 'Yes, Tedric, I do.'

So at least Carey had recognised him, which was definitely a sign of improvement. Tedric turned. His whipsword out and ready, Fra Villion stood waiting in the middle of the room. The other *vemplars* now crowded around the walls to watch. Tedric came forward. He clicked the button in the sword handle and unleashed the blade.

Villion advanced. Tedric advanced.

Villion swung first. The thrust was a tentative one, and Tedric, ducking quickly, accepted it as such. Standing upright, he replied in kind, but before his sword blade even came close to reaching Fra Villion, there was only empty space in front of him. Villion had vanished.

Tedric concentrated. He dropped to his knees. The whistling in his ears was painful in its intensity. Villion's blade cut a horizontal path through the air a bare inch above the top of Tedric's skull. Using the same power he had discovered in space while eluding the *vemplar* ships, Tedric had known in advance exactly where Villion would reappear and how he would swing his blade.

Tedric spun on his heels and lashed out at Villion, but again, before the blade reached its target, the black knight vanished. This time, he reappeared a few yards behind where he had previously stood.

Grinning at Tedric, Villion said, 'Do you wish to surrender and accept your fate?'

Tedric shook his head stubbornly. 'I thought this was a duel to the death.'

'Your death, you mean.'

'Time will answer that.'

In spite of his apparent confidence, Tedric had indeed been taken by surprise by the intensity of Villion's initial assault. Still, with his ability to know Villion's moves in advance, he felt few doubts about his own chances. He could win this duel – and he would.

Cautiously, Tedric came to his feet. He wanted to give the appearance of someone in a state of numbed shock. He concentrated on Pal Galmain's whispered revelation of Villion's one major weakness: *It's the unorthodox, Tedric,* the dying knight had revealed. *If you do what you're supposed to do, no matter how well, Villion will win. You have to do what you're not supposed to do and catch him by surprise.*

So Tedric jumped. It was the most unorthodox manoeuvre he could think of at the time. Holding his sword over his head, he dove feet first through the air. Pal Galmain was proved right. Villion's face reflected his disbelief. Tedric's boots struck him solidly in the chest and sent him tumbling to the floor. Villion's head hit hard.

Tedric came to his feet and unleashed a hard swing. Villion, recovering just in time, held up his hand and caught Tedric's blade with the handle of his own sword. The blade whipped around the handle, but Tedric jerked quickly and the sword flew out of Villion's hand. It sailed over Tedric's head and far across the room, striking the opposite wall.

Fra Villion was disarmed. Tedric advanced. Villion laughed. Then vanished.

Tedric spun at once. Villion stood on the opposite side of the room, reclaiming his weapon. Again, the two men advanced slowly. Villion broke into a run. It wasn't strictly an unorthodox move but it nonetheless surprised Tedric. Villion swung his sword vertically so that Tedric could neither stoop nor leap to evade the blade.

With death staring him in the face, Tedric threw back his sword arm. He let go of the handle and let it fly through the air. The hard wooden handle caught Fra Villion squarely on the chin and stopped his forward motion. Tedric darted swiftly around the stunned *vemplar* and retrieved his own weapon. Standing tensely, waiting for Villion to move, he gasped for breath.

Fra Villion stood up. There was blood on his chin – bluish red and thick. Tedric discovered a matching stain on the handle of his sword.

'You fight like a madman,' said Villion admiringly.

'I fight to win,' said Tedric. But he knew that a few tricks would not be enough to vanquish a swordsman as deft as Fra Villion. If he wanted to win, he would have to close with his opponent and match strength against strength. He jerked his wrist. Fra Villion responded in kind.

Standing far apart, the two men clashed swords. The blades met, touched, struck sparks. The action was so fast and the blades such blurs of motion that it was nearly impossible for the eye to follow. Tedric felt the sweat streaming down his face. This dance of parry-and-thrust was orthodox but essential. He had to prove to Fra Villion that he was his equal in the art of swordsmanship, but one slip, one occasion when his blade failed to meet Villion's, and he would die.

A thundering noise threatened to break his concentration. It took Tedric a moment to identify the sound. Applause.

The knights of Tavera were expressing their genuine admiration for what they were watching.

Villion smiled grimly, and then he disappeared. Ignoring the applause, Tedric concentrated. He turned. As orthodox in his strategy as ever, Villion had materialised behind him. Tedric leaped in the air as Villion's blade swept under his feet.

Tedric realised that sometimes the most unorthodox manoeuvre could be one that was orthodox but unexpected. So he charged Villion. Caught by surprise, the knight never had a chance to pull his vanishing act. Tedric closed with him. Their wrists slammed together and locked, blades hanging limply. Villion's strength was enormous. Tedric matched it. Their faces were mere inches apart.

His muscles bulging tautly with the strain, Tedric took a lunging step forward. Villion staggered back. Another step. Another stagger.

Villion's eyes were large in his head. He could have escaped by vanishing, Tedric knew, but his pride refused to let him run. Step by step, Tedric drove Villion back to the wall.

'Surrender,' Tedric gasped but loudly enough so that all the room could hear.

Villion shook his head silently. It was a stalemate. Realising this, Tedric jumped back. Villion swung his sword. Tedric parried the blow. Then he heard a scream of anguish.

Turning, he saw a body standing near the wall. The neck was a splash of blood. As Tedric watched, the body toppled soundlessly to the floor. It was Matthew Carey.

Dropping his sword, Tedric ran across the room. Villion could have killed him then. He did not. Why, Tedric never knew, but he could guess. Somewhere in his soul, where it mattered, Fra Villion retained the integrity of his code.

Reaching Carey, Tedric crouched and turned the body over. The throat was cut from ear to ear. Carey was dead. Standing, Tedric shook his head in disgust. 'How did it happen? Who . . .?'

Juvi pointed to a youthful-looking *vemplar* standing

nearby. The knight held an open whipsword in one hand. The blade dripped blood.

'The knight started to go to help Villion when you had him pinned against the wall,' Wilson explained. 'I was too far away to do anything, but Carey reached out and grabbed him. The knight killed Carey.'

Tedric looked down at Carey's body. It wasn't a very glorious end for a man who had once served as Emperor of Man. Still, his mind broken by Fra Villion, perhaps this had been Carey's only way of reasserting his own sense of worth.

He had saved Tedric's life. In doing so, he had died himself.

A whistle sliced the air. The head of the *vemplar* who had killed Carey slid from its shoulders and fell to the floor. For a moment, the headless body swayed, then it, too, toppled.

Fra Villion approached, his sword dangling. 'He had no right to intervene.' Villion held out a hand to Tedric. In it was Tedric's sword. 'Shall we continue?'

Tedric nodded and took the sword. He and Villion resumed their stations. Again, the blades clashed.

The duel stretched for hours. Tedric fought patiently and well. Twice, Villion broke through his guard and cut him, once on the cheek and once on his chest. Tedric did better. Villion's free arm – the left – was badly gashed from a dozen wounds. The chest of his jumpsuit was a mass of blood. His dark fur dripped red.

As the battle continued, Tedric observed Villion carefully. There was something new in the *vemplar*'s eyes. It wasn't fear. It was acceptance. Villion guessed that he was about to die, but he did not seem afraid. The two men closed, wrists locking. Villion's face pressed close to Tedric. The veins showed tautly through the blood on his forehead.

'The darker forces . . .' he whispered.

'Yes?' said Tedric.

'I was wrong to serve them. They seek the destruction of . . . of everything.'

'I know.'

137

'I never desired that. I had given my word. Once done, I could not turn back. Do you understand?'

'No.'

'It is the blood oath of the ancient code.'

'There are other codes,' said Tedric. 'More important ones.'

Villion nodded. Whether he was agreeing, Tedric could not say. Villion spun away, turned back, swung at Tedric's legs. Missing, he leaped through space, reappeared, swung immediately, missed again, then parried Tedric's return slice. The unorthodox, thought Tedric, sensing the end. I must remember to seek the unorthodox.

But Villion acted first. Duplicating Tedric's tactics, he sprang feet first through the air. Unprepared, Tedric took a crushing blow on the chest. He fell. The air burst from his lungs and his sword flew from his grasp. Alone and disarmed, Tedric lay on his back on the floor and watched as Fra Villion approached.

'So it ends,' the knight said softly.

He raised his sword to strike. Tedric shut his eyes. There was a strange singing noise in his ears. His stomach fluttered and he felt nauseous.

Then he was standing.

Opening his eyes, Tedric discovered that he stood on the opposite side of the room, staring at Villion's back. His whipsword lay at his feet. Stooping down, he retrieved it. Villion turned slowly. His eyes expressed his stunned bewilderment.

Tedric had jumped through space. But how? This was not the time to consider that. Tedric advanced, swinging his sword. Villion rushed desperately at him. The sword blades met and clashed. Tedric swung again. This time, for whatever reason, Villion failed to respond in time. Tedric's blade cut freely through the air and sliced off Villion's right ear.

Blood spurted from the skull. Tedric closed. Villion met him. Their wrists locked. Tedric gazed into Villion's eyes and saw the calm acceptance there.

'Who are they?' said Tedric. 'The darker forces – tell me.'

'I know only one,' said Villion. 'I speak with him alone.'

'I saw you in the room. I heard his voice.'

Villion looked surprised but did not ask how. 'His name . . .'

'Yes?'

'It is Sarpedion.'

'No!' cried Tedric in disbelief.

And then Villion's face altered. It was now a grinning mask. Another face – not Villion's: older, darker, more hateful. Tedric had known this face before. A long, long time ago. A place far, far from here.

Sarpedion, the dark wizard!

Tedric leaped back and swung his sword with all his might. Villion offered no resistance. His severed head flew through the air. His body fell.

Fra Villion, the black knight, was dead.

CHAPTER 17

Tedric and Skandos

Although the room was unquestionably empty, Tedric sensed that he was no longer alone. He turned his head in a futile search, then finally said, 'Skandos? Is it you?'

Tedric had returned to Earth three days before. He now stood in a bedroom in Alyc Carey's house. She, Yod Cartwright, Juvi Jerome, and Ky-shan were outside waiting for him to join them at this moment.

A gentle voice spoke in his mind: *I have come to converse with you, Tedric.*

It was Skandos all right. 'Is there . . . trouble?' Usually, when it was necessary for Skandos to speak to him, Tedric was summoned to Prime.

No, no trouble at all. You've had a long and arduous journey. I felt it kindest to allow you to continue your holiday without interruption. Besides, there are occasions when I derive pleasure from revisiting Earth, even in this rather indirect way. I lived here once, you know. I was born not more than five hundred miles from where you stand.

Tedric had not known that. The origins of the Scientists, who they were and where they came from, were buried in a misty past. 'I'm glad you've come,' he said, going to a chair and sitting down. His voice was soft. He knew it wasn't necessary to speak but found it more comfortable, easier to arrange his thoughts clearly. 'I must have a million questions to ask you.'

Skandos's amusement showed in his voice. *I'm afraid I may not be able to answer quite that many. Will three or four suffice for the moment? I followed your progress in the Bioman Sphere and was pleased by your success.*

'That's what bothers me. I succeeded but I don't know

why. During my duel with Fra Villion, I hopped through space. It just happened and I don't know how.'

In time, I think you will, said Skandos. *Remember, when I first brought you to this universe, I explained that you possessed certain unrealised powers.*

'Does that mean I'm not a normal man?' said Tedric.

You are a normal man – a man of your own universe. Tell me, how much do you recall of that other place?

'Only a very little.' Tedric shook his head. 'I've tried and tried but it's still very vague.'

It is a universe where magic works.

'Is that what I did? Was it magic?'

It was – but it wasn't. Was Villion's ability to leap through space a result of magic? No, it was only a different way of using the brain. You must learn to accept your powers and use them wisely.

Tedric knew that Skandos's evasiveness was deliberate. Through the window, he could hear the voices of Alyc, Yod and Juvi, laughing and talking. For some reason, he thought instead of Lola Dass. Keeping his promise, he had allowed her to return to Earth with them aboard a ship provided by the *vemplars*. She was somewhere in New Melbourne now. He wondered idly if he would ever see her again and found himself hoping very much that he would. Embarrassed, he cut off that thought quickly. It was very possible that Skandos could hear everything he was thinking.

Hastily, Tedric said, 'What about the red cloud? I don't understand that either. When I killed Villion without learning how to reach beyond him, I assumed I had failed. But the cloud disappeared. From what Alyc tells me, it must have disappeared the moment I killed Villion.'

It did.

'But why?'

Have you ever played chess, Tedric?

'I have, yes.'

When a piece is captured it must be removed from further play. Is that correct?

'Yes, of course.'

Well, by defeating Fra Villion you forced our adversaries to remove a piece from play – the cloud. It was part of the rules of the game, Tedric.

'And you knew this all along?'

I suspected it, yes. The rules are not always entirely clear.

'Why didn't you tell me?'

I saw no need. If you had failed and Villion lived, the cloud would certainly have swallowed up Earth. You knew this fact. I did not wish to intervene and risk a similar move by the other side.

'By Sarpedion?' As he spoke the name, Tedric again felt its familiarity.

By Sarpedion, Skandos confirmed.

'Have I known him before?' Tedric asked.

You have. Skandos seemed hesitant to proceed.

'Can you tell me when? Or where? It wasn't here. I'm sure of that. It must have been in the other universe.'

Skandos seemed to make a decision. *I can tell you certain things about Sarpedion and shall, but you must not ask me to elucidate – not at this time.*

'I understand,' said Tedric.

Sarpedion is a man – in the same sense that I am a man. Once he was a Scientist and dwelled among his colleagues on Prime. He was an able man but one driven by a lust for power. In time that lust came to dominate his personality. He inserted himself directly into the affairs of another universe. It was your universe, Tedric – and he acted as if he were a god. When his crime was discovered, he was brought to trial and sentenced to permanent exile. Later, he joined our adversaries in search of revenge – against us and against you.

Tedric had to resist the urge to ask Skandos any of a dozen obvious questions. He sighed. 'Is that all you can tell me?'

That and the fact that he is our supreme enemy. No one stands behind him, though there are many at his side. For eons, our adversaries lay dormant. Now they are on the move again and they will not rest until we – or they – are forever vanquished.

'But where are they? Why have I never seen them?'

Few men have. But they exist. Their planet lies in a distant part of this galaxy.

'Then I must go there,' said Tedric.

Skandos laughed. *In time – in good time. That will have to wait for later. For now we must concentrate upon the threat of the clouds. One is gone but others remain.*

Tedric nodded thoughtfully. He opened his mouth to ask another question, then realised something. He was alone. Skandos had gone.

With a bemused sigh, Tedric went slowly to the bedroom window and drew back the thin curtain. Outside, Alyc, Yod and Juvi ran back and forth on a small patch of green lawn, playing catch with a round rubber ball. Tedric watched Alyc, marvelling at the way, though blind, she always seemed to know exactly where the ball was coming from. She never hesitated, never wavered, never faltered.

He turned away. No, it wasn't magic. It wasn't magic for Alyc or for Villion or for himself.

What it was and how it could be used to save the universe from the threat of Sarpedion was something he would have to find out. When? He shrugged and turned for the door.

Only time could answer that question.

Wyndham Books are obtainable from many booksellers and newsagents. If you have any difficulty please send purchase price plus postage on the scale below to:

Wyndham Cash Sales
P.O. Box 11
Falmouth
Cornwall
OR
Star Book Service,
G.P.O. Box 29,
Douglas,
Isle of Man,
British Isles.

While every effort is made to keep prices low, it is sometimes necessary to increase prices at short notice. Wyndham Books reserve the right to show new retail prices on covers which may differ from those advertised in the text or elsewhere.

Postage and Packing Rate

UK: 30p for the first book, plus 15p per copy for each additional book ordered to a maximum charge of £1.29.
BFPO and Eire: 30p for the first book, plus 15p per copy for the next 6 books and thereafter 6p per book.
Overseas: 50p for the first book and 15p per copy for each additional book.

These charges are subject to Post Office charge fluctuations.